For more than forty years,
Yearling has been the leading name
in classic and award-winning literature
for young readers.

Yearling books feature children's
favorite authors and characters,
providing dynamic stories of adventure,
humor, history, mystery, and fantasy.

Trust Yearling paperbacks to entertain,
inspire, and promote the love of reading
in all children.

OTHER YEARLING BOOKS YOU WILL ENJOY

BILLY CLIKK: CREATCH BATTLER, *Mark Crilley*

BOBBY BASEBALL, *Robert Kimmel Smith*

BOYS AGAINST GIRLS, *Phyllis Reynolds Naylor*

DOGS DON'T TELL JOKES, *Louis Sachar*

HOLES, *Louis Sachar*

HARRIET SPIES AGAIN, *Louise Fitzhugh and Helen Ericson*

HOW ANGEL PETERSON GOT HIS NAME, *Gary Paulsen*

NICKY DEUCE
Welcome to the Family

STEVEN R. SCHIRRIPA & CHARLES FLEMING

A Yearling Book

Published by Yearling, an imprint of Random House Children's Books
a division of Random House, Inc., New York

Visit us on the Web! www.randomhouse.com/kids
Educators and librarians, for a variety of teaching tools, visit us at
www.randomhouse.com/teachers

ISBN-13: 978-0-440-42053-8
ISBN-10: 0-440-42053-9

Reprinted by arrangement with Delacorte Press
Printed in the United States of America
November 2006
10 9 8 7 6 5 4 3 2 1

For the loves of my life, Laura, Bria, Ciara and my mom, Lorraine
                                                                    —S.S.

To my daughters, Katie and Frankie, for giving me their help in writ-ing this book, and to my wife, Julie Singer, for giving me daughters
                                                                    —C.F.

Steve Schirripa would like to thank David Vigliano, Beverly Horowitz, Pam Krauss, Johnny Planco, Allison Walker, Roger Haber, Lisa Perkins, Cheryl McLean, Valerie Baugh, Alexandria Addams, all my friends in Bensonhurst (you know who you are) and my good pal Charles Fleming.

Charles Fleming would like to thank the honorary goombas Beverly Horowitz, Pam Krauss and David Vigliano, and the orig-inal goomba, Steve Schirripa.

CHAPTER ONE

The big black Lincoln Navigator rolled slowly down Bath Avenue. A group of teenage boys playing stickball in the street stopped their game and stared. The huge SUV had smoked black windows and, one of the boys saw through the windshield, a uniformed black driver.

"Hey—it's a limo!" the boy shouted.

The ragtag group of boys circled the car. They pressed their hands and faces against the windows and stared inside.

"What's the big idea, breaking up our game?" one of them shouted.

"Hey, mister, who's the celebrity?" another yelled.

"Open up and let us see!" a third said.

Soon the boys were banging their hands on the side of the SUV and chanting, "Open up and let us see! Open up and let us see!"

The Navigator came to a stop at the curb. Then the driver's-side door swung open. The uniformed driver, menacing in his mirrored sunglasses and chauffeur's hat, said, "All right, boys. *Back off*."

The crowd of boys went silent—for a second—and then began chanting again. The driver scowled and studied the numbers on the houses.

In the back of the Navigator sat twelve-year-old Nicholas Borelli II. He was pale and thin and wore khaki pants, a polo shirt and a dark blue sports coat with a school emblem over the pocket. He watched the chanting boys with dread. He'd been right all along: he did not want to go to Brooklyn.

He was supposed to be at Camp Wannameka. The night before he was to leave, though, there'd been a phone call. Nicholas was in his room at home in the leafy suburb of Carrington, New Jersey, packing his things in a duffel bag. In went the swimsuit, the sunscreen, the snorkel, the digital camera, the Game Boy, the cell phone and his pencils and sketch pad—filled with drawings of his camp friends at play. Noah at the archery range. Chad and Jordan in a canoe. Noah and Chad and Jordan after a lacrosse match.

The next morning his father's man, Clarence, would drive him two hours north into upstate New York. For three weeks, Nicholas would run, swim, sail, fish, canoe and drink watery fruit juice.

But then the phone rang. Nicholas strained to hear what was being said. He went downstairs. He found his parents in the kitchen. They wouldn't look him in the eye.

"There's been an accident at Camp Wannameka," his father said. "An explosion in the septic system. The entire camp is knee-deep in, uh, sewage. Camp is canceled."

"Camp Wannameka is knee-deep in crapola?" Nicholas said.

"Nicholas!" his mother exclaimed.

"Sorry," he said. "Are you going to cancel your cruise?"

"We're leaving tomorrow morning, just as scheduled," Nicholas' father said. "You're going to spend the next couple of weeks with your grandmother."

"Grandma Tutti is coming here?"

"You're going to stay with *her*, Nicholas," his mother said. "Clarence will drive you to New York. To . . . Brooklyn."

Brooklyn! Brooklyn? Nobody went to Brooklyn!

Brooklyn was the place where his father had grown up. Brooklyn was full of Italians—the people his father called *goombas*. Brooklyn was the place his father hated most in the world.

"Forget it," Nicholas said, and ran to his room. "I'm not going."

But here he was. Nicholas looked through the smoked black windows, past the chanting boys. The street was lined with three-story brick buildings. Some of them had businesses on the ground floor and apartments above. Nicholas could see a butcher shop, and a candy store, and a dry cleaner. Music came from open windows. The heat was stifling.

Clarence opened the back door and pulled out Nicholas' duffel bag.

One of the boys said, "He's coming out!"

Another said, "Somebody call the newspapers!"

Another said, "Somebody get the red carpet!"

Nicholas stepped onto the street.

One of the boys said, "Hey, it's nobody!"

Another said, "It's just some rich kid!"

"Hey, rich kid! Gimme ten bucks!"

The boys crowded around. Clarence put his arm around Nicholas' shoulders. The boys started chanting, "Gimme ten bucks! Gimme ten bucks!"

Then a voice said, "You boys! Stop it!" and the crowd went silent.

Nicholas' grandmother was on the street. She was short and compact and dressed in a black cotton housedress, and she was carrying a long wooden spoon.

"You, Tommy! You, Angelo! Get away from here before I call your mothers."

The boys scattered. Nicholas' grandmother smiled and opened her arms. She said, "Nicky! *Caro mio!*" and gave him a huge hug. "I'm so glad you're here. Come inside. Who's the African?"

"The what?"

"The airline pilot. With the bags."

"That's Clarence, Grandma. He's Dad's driver."

"Ask him if he wants to come inside," she said, and then shouted, "Do-you-want-to-come-inside?"

"Mr. Borelli instructed me to—"

"*Capito,*" Grandma Tutti said with finality. "Just bring the bags."

It was five steps up the broad concrete stoop, through a short hallway, then into a dark, cool apartment that smelled like bread, garlic and old people. Nicholas' grandmother said, "Your room is at the end of the hall, on the left. Put the bags in there."

Nicholas followed Clarence to a room with a single

bed and a small desk. On the walls were posters and pictures and sports pennants. Nicholas stared at a black-
and-white photograph of two young men. One was a
husky kid wearing a baseball uniform and cap. The
other was a thin, nerdy-looking kid wearing glasses and
a sports coat.

"Clarence, look! It's Dad."

Clarence peered at the picture and whistled. "So it
is. I bet this is your dad's old room."

Nicholas' grandmother was waiting with her purse.
She said, "How much do we owe you?"

"Nothing at all, ma'am. Mr. Borelli said—well,
goodbye, Nicholas. Good luck."

Clarence shook Nicholas' hand gravely, bowed to
Nicholas' grandmother and left them.

Nicholas looked at his grandmother. She looked at
him. She said, "Skin and bones. Just like your father!
Go wash your hands, and then come and help me in the
kitchen."

His grandmother was stirring a pot of sauce with the
large wooden spoon she'd used to scare away the
teenagers in the street. Nicholas could smell garlic and
tomato. In a frying pan were balls of something that
looked like hamburger.

"I'm making meatballs," Nicholas' grandmother

said. "It was your father's favorite. Does your mother cook that for you?"

"No. She doesn't cook Italian food at all."

"*Allora*, what can you expect? She's not Italian like us. Never mind. So, I'll teach you. Take this spoon, and stir around in circles like this."

Nicholas stood next to the stove and began stirring. His grandmother pushed the meatballs around in the frying pan.

"I didn't tell your mother and father, because it would only have started a fight, but your uncle is living here, too, now. His wife—the good-for-nothing—she threw him out. Stir the sauce."

Nicholas made some more circles in the sauce.

"Well, good riddance. I said it was a mistake from the beginning. At least she's Italian—not like your mother, God bless her, she's a wonderful woman, but why couldn't your father marry a nice girl from the neighborhood?—but she's never been any good. Have a meatball."

"Yes, Grandmother."

"Don't call me Grandmother. Call me Tutti. Here."

She stretched out her spoon toward Nicholas. He took the piece of meat with his fingers and popped it into his mouth.

Nicholas' mother was a vegetarian. This was the

first meatball he had ever tasted. It was the most delicious thing he'd ever eaten in his life. So he reached for another.

Smack! His grandmother swung the wooden spoon onto the back of his hand.

"For later," she said. "Anyway, here comes Frankie."

CHAPTER TWO

He was a big man, tall and wide. He had thick black hair and heavy black eyebrows. He was wearing a jogging suit, and a gold watch, and a gold chain around his neck. He dropped a gym bag in the hallway and started toward the kitchen. He wasn't smiling. He looked tired. He was staring at Nicholas.

"Hey, Ma. Who's the kid?"

"It's Nicholas."

"Nicholas what?"

"Don't be an idiot. Your nephew Nicholas."

"This?" The big man smiled. "This is little Nicky? Hey, kid! How ya doin'?"

Nicholas stood up and extended his hand. Frankie grabbed it and pulled Nicholas to him and hugged him to his chest.

"You used to be such a shrimp, and look at you now!" Frankie said, holding the boy at arm's length. "All grown up, sort of. Where's your father?"

"He didn't come," his mother said. "He sent a car. Mr. Big Shot, too busy to visit his own mother."

"Ah, you know it's not like that, Ma," Frankie said. "But what's the kid doing here?"

"He's staying here," Tutti said. "His mother and father are going on a cruise. Nicky was supposed to go to summer camp, but the toilet exploded—don't ask me. So Nicky's staying here in his dad's old room."

"Spending the summer in Bensonhurst!" Frankie said. "Did you eat already? Did she give you something?"

"I had a meatball."

"Just one, right? You can never get more than one!"

Frankie reached for the pan, but out came the spoon again—fast! Grandma Tutti got him on the back of the hand.

"One meatball!" Frankie yelped. "One!"

"Out!" his mother said. "Dinner's in an hour. Take down the garbage."

"Come on, kid," Frankie said. "Let's get out of here."

Frankie reached under the sink, pulled out a sack of garbage and led Nicholas back down the hall, out the front door and down the stoop. The trash bins were be-hind the building.

"Now that you're living here, this is your job," Frankie said. "Every day, you gotta take the trash down. Got it?"

"Sure thing," Nicholas said.

Frankie put the top back on the trash can. He ges-tured at the street, which was empty now.

"Did you already see the neighborhood?"

"A little," Nicholas said.

"Isn't it great? In the summer, it's the best! You got stickball, slapball, Johnny on a pony, hit the stick, ring-a-levio . . ."

"That sounds like a skin disease. Is it a game?"

"They're all games! You play stickball with a thing like a broomstick and a ball called a spaldeen. And Johnny on a pony—you'll see. There's a lot of kids your age here. I'll show you around. You'll make some friends."

Nicholas remembered the crowd he'd seen around the Navigator. He didn't think he'd make friends with any of that group. He followed Frankie inside, to a fam-ily room at the back of the apartment. Frankie flopped down onto an easy chair. There was a television in the corner. On one wall was a large crucifix, with rosary beads hanging over it. On another there were framed pictures of Frank Sinatra and the Pope.

Nicholas said, "You guys know Frank Sinatra?"

"Not personally," Frankie said. "We don't know the Pope that well, either. But I almost met Frank one time. He was part of this parade. Me and a bunch of guys tricked old man Fornelli, the guy that owned the corner grocery store. We went inside like we were going to buy a soda. When the parade started, Mikey said, 'Hey! It's Frank Sinatra!' Mr. Fornelli ran outside. Mikey closed the door and locked it. We got Italian sandwiches and went up to the second floor. We ate the sandwiches and watched the parade while Mr. Fornelli pounded on the door, trying to get inside. Beautiful!"

"So what happened?"

"Nothing. We screamed, 'Frank! Frank!' but he didn't even wave."

"Didn't you get in trouble?"

"Trouble? *Fugheddaboudit*. I never got into trouble. I just caused trouble. It usually involved food. One summer we figured out how to get free pizza. I'd call and order a pizza to be delivered to, say, 161 Bath Avenue, apartment 1-A. Then another guy would call and order another pizza for 201 Bath Avenue, apartment 2-B. Both of the addresses were phony, but the pizza guy didn't know that. So he'd drive into the neighborhood and park the car and take a pizza into 161 Bath Avenue. We'd swoop down and steal the other pizza right out of the back of his car. Free pizza!"

"You never got caught?"

"Never! Because we were smart. We never hit any pizzerias run by Italians. We stayed away from the wiseguy places. That's the lesson. You cross a wiseguy, you're history. Never forget that."

"Okay," Nicholas said. "What's a wiseguy?"

"Oh boy," Frankie said. "You got a lot to learn. But let's eat first."

In addition to the meatballs and rigatoni, Tutti had prepared some kind of chicken and some kind of cooked vegetable that looked like salad.

"What a feast!" Frankie said as they sat down. "Roast chicken, and escarole. *And* the meatballs. Pass the macaroni."

Frankie ate with gusto. Nicholas could see how he'd gotten so big. He ate big—two pieces of chicken, a huge plate of rigatoni and meatballs and some escarole.

"That's some meal, Ma," Frankie said. "I bet the kid don't eat like this at home, huh?"

"Not exactly," Nicholas said. "My mom's a vegetarian. And she's always on a diet."

"Well, you can forget the diet around here. As long as Ma's cooking, no one's going on any diets. Right, Ma?"

Grandma Tutti shrugged. "I cook what I like to eat," she said. "But it's nice to have two men at the table again. Not since your father died, and your brother left . . ."

Frankie stared into his empty plate. Grandma Tutti

pulled a wad of Kleenex from her sleeve and dabbed her eyes.

"That's about enough of that," Frankie said. "What's for dessert?"

"I bought some cannoli," Grandma Tutti said. "I'll make a little coffee."

Nicholas got up and started taking plates and glasses to the sink. Frankie stared at him.

"What are you doing?"

"I'm clearing the table," Nicholas said.

"Oh, no you don't," Frankie said. "This goomba ain't doing no dishes. The kitchen is your grandmother's place. Come with me."

Nicholas followed his uncle down the hall to the room with the easy chair in it. Frankie flopped down, undid the belt on his trousers and said, "What a meal. I'm stuffed. So, how's your old man doing? He working hard?"

"That's all he does, is work hard."

"He's very ambitious, your dad," Frankie said. "He was always a hard worker. In school, after school, studying . . . He left for college and he never looked back. Me, I like to take a rest now and then."

"Frankie!" Grandma Tutti's voice came sharply down the hall. "The sink! How many times I gotta ask you?"

Frankie stood up and said, "So much for the rest. C'mon. We got chores."

Frankie went to a hall closet and pulled out a toolbox, then led Nicholas to the bathroom. He opened the toolbox and took out a pair of wrenches and a flashlight.

"This sink is leaking again," he said. "Let's see what we can do."

He lay on the floor, covering most of it, and said, "Gimme that big wrench."

"You said *goomba*," Nicholas said. "What is that?"

"You don't know what's a goomba? Doesn't your old man teach you anything?"

"Not anything Italian."

"All right," Frankie said. "A goomba is, like—me. A goomba is an Italian—an Italian-American—from New York, or New Jersey, or maybe Buffalo. He's a guy from the neighborhood. They probably don't have any goombas up where you live in Caramel Town."

"Carrington."

"Whatever. A goomba is a guy who's been around. He knows a few things. He didn't go to the university, like your old man, but he ain't stupid. And he ain't a crook, either. He may know some goodfellas, but he's no wiseguy. You got that?"

"Sort of," Nicholas said. "What's a goodfella?"

"Oh boy," Frankie said, and slid out from under the sink. "You've seen *The Godfather*, right?"

"No. My dad wouldn't let me."

"No *Godfather*! That's your heritage! You're an Italian—well, half Italian, anyway. Did you see *Raging Bull*?"

"No."

"*Goodfellas*?"

"No."

"Do you watch *The Sopranos*?"

"My parents won't let me. But I saw one episode at a friend's house."

"They won't let you? This is barbaric! What about *Rocky*, at least?"

"Yeah. I saw *Rocky*."

"All right, then. That's a goomba. Rocky Balboa is a goomba. *Now* you get it?"

"I guess."

"We're going to watch *The Godfather*, right away. You need an education."

An hour later, Grandma Tutti, Frankie and Nicholas had their dessert in the family room. Biting off the end of a cannoli, Frankie said, "I remember another time I got in trouble. Me and some guys met this nut who was passing phony twenty-dollar bills. This guy would sell us brand-new twenties for five bucks. We'd buy one each, and then make 'em look old—soak 'em in skin cream, bake 'em on the radiator and wrinkle 'em up.

Then we'd take them to a candy store or an ice cream shop. We'd buy something that cost a dollar, and get nineteen dollars in change. Bingo! Free money!"

"You're a bad influence," Grandma Tutti said.

"I'm teaching him a lesson," Frankie said. "The thing is, not like the pizza thing, this was *stupid*. Passing bad bills is a serious crime. You can go to jail for a long time for that."

"Did you go to jail?"

"No. I was lucky, and I didn't get caught. But the guy that was selling us the bills, he went away for five years. We never saw him again. He got killed in a robbery."

"Wow."

"Exactly," Frankie said. "So let that be a lesson to you. Don't do something stupid!"

"Francis! You're turning Nicholas into a hoodlum!"

"Nah, Ma, I'm just wising him up to the neighborhood," Frankie said. "Speaking of which . . . Not for nothing, but *Nicholas* doesn't sound right. What do your friends call you?"

"Nicholas," said Nicholas.

"That's no good. It may sound right up there in Carriage Town, but it don't sound right in Brooklyn. From now on, you're Nicky. Or Nicky B. Or, since you're Nicholas Borelli the Second—after your father—how about Nicky Two? No! *Nicky Deuce*. That's a good name for a junior goomba. How about we call you Nicky Deuce?"

"Yeah," Nicky said. "That's good."

"All right, Nicky Deuce. Now, *The Godfather*. You got a lot to learn."

CHAPTER THREE

$\mathcal{N}$icky was up early the following morning. The apartment was silent. Nicky sat alone with his sketch pad, drawing Grandma Tutti standing over the stove. He was still sketching when Frankie came in wearing boxer shorts and a sleeveless undershirt.

"Hey, kid," Frankie said. "What's that?"

"Nothing," Nicky said. "I'm just fooling around."

"Lemme see." Nicky handed the pad to his uncle. Frankie whistled. "That ain't bad, kid. Listen, there's a couple of bucks on my dresser. Go down to the candy store on the corner and get a newspaper, will you?"

"Which corner?"

"The one that way," Frankie said, and pointed. "Introduce yourself and tell Mikey it's for me."

Nicky put his shoes on and went down the hall to Frankie's room.

It was larger than Nicky's. There were heavy shades on the window, and it was very dark. Nicky bumped his shin on the gym bag he'd seen Frankie come home with the night before. It felt like big hunks of metal were in there. Nicky found the dresser, and the money, and went down to the street.

Moms were pushing strollers, heading for the market. Men in suits were going to work. Old ladies sat in their windows, staring down at the street.

Nicky went to the corner store. The shop was called Mazzetta's. Inside, there were cold drinks, and candy and snacks, and newspapers and cigarettes. The guy behind the counter wore an apron and had a pencil stuck behind his ear.

Nicky said, "Are you Mikey?"

"Who wants to know?"

"My name is Nicholas Borelli. My uncle Frankie sent me down for the newspaper."

"Nicholas Borelli? You're Nicky's kid?"

"Yes, sir."

"Yes, sir? Get a load of you! How's Nicky doing? How's your dad?"

"He's okay."

"How come he don't come down here no more?"

"I don't know."

"I haven't seen him since high school. What a brain! He was a little genius! I remember when he got married— not that I got invited to the wedding, but still. That would be your mother, right?"

"I guess so."

"You tell Nicky that Mikey said hello. It's a dollar for the paper."

Back at the apartment, sitting on the stoop, was an elderly man wearing a black suit and smoking a cigarette. He appeared to be asleep: his chin was on his chest, and he was snoring. Nicky stepped around him and went upstairs.

His grandmother was up now. The kitchen smelled like coffee, and she was frying sausage.

"Your uncle is in the shower," she said. "Give me a kiss and sit down. How do you like your eggs— scrambled?"

"I don't know," Nicky said. "I don't usually eat eggs."

"No eggs? Here, you get them scrambled. Sit."

Nicky set down the newspaper and said, "There's an old man sleeping on the front steps. He smells funny."

"He's drunk," Grandma Tutti said. "His name is Moretti. He lives in the basement apartment. He was a friend of your grandfather's, from the war. He moved in here in 1955. He never left."

"He was asleep, but he was also smoking a cigarette."

"He's drunk, like I said," Grandma Tutti said. "Don't pay any attention to him. He won't hurt you."

Frankie came into the kitchen wearing a fancier tracksuit than he'd been wearing the night before and said, "Let's take a walk."

Everyone knew Frankie. On every corner, in every shop, at every door, someone said, "Morning, Frank," or, "Yo, Frank-o," or, "Heya, Frankie-boy." Every time someone new said hello, Frankie would stop, put his arm around Nicky's shoulder and say, "Howya doon? This here's Nicky Deuce, my nephew from the suburbs."

Farther up the block there was an enormous fat guy sitting on a lawn chair next to his car. The trunk was open, and the smell of hot dogs filled the air.

"That's Fat Farouk Junior," Frankie said. "I used to buy hot dogs from his dad, when I was a kid. Fat Farouk had four sons. One became a priest. One became a mailman. One became a wiseguy. And Fat Farouk Junior took over the family business. Hey, Farouk!"

Fat Farouk raised a fat hand and waved. "Heya, Frankie. How's it going?"

Along the way, Frankie showed Nicky the neighborhood. Next to the candy store was a barbershop. Across the street was the drugstore. On the next block was the laundry. Across the street from that was the beauty parlor. Next to it was the Italian deli.

"Very important," Frankie said. "This is your *sala-maria*. This is where you go for sausages and cheeses, your cold cuts, your pepperoni and your mortadella. No place else. This is run by Italians. You can trust the food here."

"Don't you ever go to, like, Super Buy or City Market?"

"Only for stuff you don't eat, like toilet paper, or soap," Frankie said. "If it's something you're going to eat, you get it from people you know. Mozzarella from the supermarket? I skeeve that."

"Skeeve?"

"Yeah. It's skeevy. It's disgusting to me."

Halfway down the block there was a policeman writing out parking tickets and sticking them on windshields.

But there was something wrong with the policeman. His uniform was too small. The pants ended about five inches above his ankles, and his wrists stuck out from the sleeves. The badge pinned to his chest looked like a dime store sheriff's badge. On his feet were enormous white basketball shoes without laces.

When they were close to him, Frankie said, "Hey, Nutty. Writing some tickets?"

"Writing some tickets—yep, Frankie."

"Good for you, Nut."

A half block on, Nicky said, "Okay. What was that?"

"What?"

"That policeman."

"That was Nutty. He's a neighborhood guy. He likes to dress up and do stuff on the block. Today, he's a cop."

"Does everyone know he's not a real policeman?"

"Everybody knows Nutty," Frankie said. "He's lived here his whole life. People love Nutty."

On the next block they stopped at a storefront with the words "Bath Avenue Social Club" written on the door. Frankie said, "Come on. I'll introduce you to some people."

Inside, a man was slicing bread rolls. Five men in suits were sitting at tables, playing cards and smoking cigars. One of them looked up and said, "Hey, Frankie," and the others turned and said hello.

"Hey, you bums. Meet my nephew, Nicky. He's from the suburbs. I'm turning him into a goomba."

Nicky went around shaking hands.

"This is Sallie the Butcher, Jimmy the Iceman and Oscar the Undertaker," Frankie said. "That's Charlie Cement, and Bobby Car Service. Behind the counter, that's Eddie."

Eddie said, "You want a sangwich, kid?"

Nicky said, "No, thanks. I just had breakfast."

"Sit down," Frankie said. "You can eat a sandwich. And a coffee for me, Eddie."

The conversation went fast and was hard to follow.

The men talked about sports, and horses, and going to the track.

Charlie Cement said, "I told Allie Bags, 'Give me the Giants a hundred times.' He says, 'You're into me too much already. No more bets till you pay.' Can you believe the guy? Five years I'm making book with him. I owe him a grand. What am I gonna do, rob a bank?"

"You shoulda went to see Ronnie Mack," said Sallie the Butcher.

"What do you think I did? I went to see Ronnie Mack. He gave me the Giants *two hundred times*. The Giants win, and I pay off Allie Bags. He says, 'Whatta you want for the Saints on Sunday?' I said, 'I want another bookie, you tightwad.'"

"He *is* a tightwad," Frankie said. "I've known the guy twenty years. You ever see him pick up a check?"

"He's got alligator arms," Sallie the Butcher said. "They don't reach all the way to his pockets."

"Somebody ought to knock some sense into that guy," said Jimmy the Iceman.

When they got back to the apartment, Frankie said, "I got to get to work," and left Nicky with his grandmother.

"We're going shopping," she said. "Then we'll have a little lunch."

Nicky had been shopping plenty of times with his

mother. They'd drive to the Super Buy and walk up and down the aisles, filling their cart. They'd buy the same things every week—cauliflower, broccoli, potatoes, bananas, tofu . . . They were back in the car in half an hour.

That wasn't how Grandma Tutti shopped. She had a little pull-along cart. On the way, she stopped every five feet to chat. She knew *everybody*. She waved to old women sitting in their windows on the second floor. She talked to old women sitting on the front stoops. She looked in at the flower shop and the beauty salon. She waved through the glass at the barbershop and the corner store.

And she bought her groceries from about six different stores. She went to the *salamaria* for sausages and mozzarella cheese. But she went to the cheese store for the parmesan. "You can't trust the *salamaria* for the parmesan," she said. "It's sometimes not fresh."

They went to a fruit store for pears and grapes. They went to a different store for cannellini beans, broccoli, garlic, lettuce and arugula. She spent a long time picking out two red and two green bell peppers.

When they were done at last, Grandma Tutti said, "Now we'll go to the market. I need canned tomatoes and paper towels."

* * *

Back at the apartment, Nicky sat with his sketch pad, drawing and talking while his grandmother cooked. She was very slow in the kitchen, and very meticulous. She sliced her garlic razor-thin. She pressed her tomatoes through a strainer to remove the skins and seeds. She roasted the bell peppers, browned the sausages and talked.

"Your grandfather's family knew my family from the old country. They were very poor. Your grandfather came to this country to try to make money. I met him here, at a dance. He was very handsome and charming. Go get the picture from the living room."

Nicky took down the portrait of his grandfather—a handsome man with a bristly mustache and twinkly eyes. Nicky sat down across from the picture and began sketching his grandfather.

"There, you see? Handsome!" his grandmother said. "Also, a very good dancer. Ten years older than me. He was very smart, but uneducated. So he was a bricklayer all his life."

Grandma Tutti stirred her sausages for a long time. She said, "He was ashamed of not having an education. That's why he wanted your father and your uncle to go to college. With Frankie, in the end, it didn't work out so good like with your father."

"Why not?"

"Frankie wasn't book-smart. But he was a fine athlete. He was on the football team and the baseball team and the track team. He got many offers of scholarships. In the end, he decided on UCLA. But that summer, working with your grandfather, he had his accident and—*pfffft!* No college."

"What accident?"

Grandma Tutti wiped her hands on her apron and sat down across from Nicky. "Your grandfather had a big job in New Jersey. He was building the fireplace and the chimney. He was not so young anymore, so Frankie was helping him. This made your father very jealous. He wanted to help, too. But your grandfather said, 'Stay home and study!' He was too little."

"He's still not as big as Uncle Frankie."

"Exactly. So one day the bricks were being delivered. Something happened, and a load of bricks got loose. Frankie was downstairs, and some of the bricks fell on him. His foot was crushed. For a while, they didn't know if they could save it. He was on crutches for almost a year. The scholarships—gone! He stayed home until he got married, to that no-good runaround. Ah! Let me see your picture."

Nicky handed over his sketch pad.

"You made the eyes too small," Tutti said. "But it looks like him. Maybe you could have a scholarship, too—for art."

* * *

That night, after another huge dinner, Uncle Frankie took out a stack of DVDs and said, "I'm gonna show you a whole bunch of goomba stuff. Siddown."

Frankie played the scene from *Mickey Blue Eyes* where they try to teach Hugh Grant how to be a goomba and say *"Fugheddaboudit."* He can't do it. He can only say "Forget *aboouuout* it" or "Forget about *it.*"

He played the scene from *Analyze This* where Billy Crystal pretends to be a gangster. He doesn't speak Italian, but he shouts out greetings that make him sound like a goomba: "Hey!" "Eee!" "Ai!" "Oh!" "You!"

He played the scene from *Taxi Driver* where Robert De Niro stares down his imaginary enemy in the mirror. "You talking to me? You talking to me? I'm the only one here. . . ."

They watched an episode of *The Sopranos*, the one where Christopher and Paulie Walnuts get lost in the snow and the woods. Frankie laughed so hard Nicky thought he was going to pop.

When it was over, Uncle Frankie said, "There you go. That's your goomba. You can see he's a pretty tough guy, right? He's a man. He's not afraid to fight. He's not afraid to stand up for himself. He likes to eat, and he likes to talk, and he likes to chase girls. You like *that*, right?"

"Well, I haven't really—"

"*Fugheddaboudit.* You're only twelve. That's for later. The point is, the goomba is loyal, and he sticks by his pals, and he's no quitter. He'd never betray a friend. That's the goomba code. The goomba is an honorable man—whether he's a gangster or a lawyer or a cop."

"A goomba could be a cop?"

"Sure! A couple of goomba kids I used to run with, they grew up to be cops."

"But most of your friends, they grew up to be other stuff, right?"

"Sure. They do all kinds of stuff."

"Are most of them gangsters?"

Uncle Frankie gave Nicky a look. "My friends? Are you kidding? They have regular jobs."

"What about you?"

"What about me what?"

"What do you do?"

"Me? I keep an eye on things for some people."

"You mean, like, a security guard?"

"Something like that, yeah," Frankie said. "Sorta like a security guard. Let's go get an ice cream."

The streets were filled with people—kids running around, older people standing and talking, or sitting on their stoops. At the corner, taking up the whole intersection, a pack of boys was playing a game that looked like baseball, but without the bat.

"That's slapball," Frankie said. "And up there, on the corner, there's a true-blue goomba. You see the fat guy with the cigar?"

"Yes."

"That's the neighborhood *patrone*. Everyone calls him Little Johnny Vegas. You got a problem with the landlord, you go to him. You got a problem with your neighbor, you go to him. He settles all the local business—like Marlon Brando in *The Godfather*, only not so dangerous."

"How does he make a living?"

"Who knows?" Frankie said. "Don't ask! I'll introduce you."

Little Johnny Vegas was huge. He needed a shave. His shoes needed a shine. His hair needed a comb. He smiled at Frankie and said, "Hey, Frankie-boy. C'mere, you gorilla," and gave him a big pat on the back.

"Johnny, this is my nephew, Nicky Deuce. He's my brother Nicky's son. He's staying with me and Ma for a few weeks."

"Nicky Deuce, huh?" Johnny stuck his hand out. "How ya doin'?"

Nicky shook hands. It was like shaking hands with a baseball mitt.

"Good-looking kid," Johnny said. "What's with the clothes?"

"I know," Frankie said. "It's Brooks Brothers."

"It looks more like Mario Brothers." Johnny stuck his hand in his pocket and pulled out an enormous bankroll. He peeled off a couple of bills and shoved them into Nicky's shirt pocket. He said, "Frankie, get the kid something decent to wear, will ya? The other kids see him in that L.L.Bean stuff, they'll tear him apart."

"Thanks, Johnny."

"*Fugheddaboudit*. Nice meeting you, kid."

When they got back to the apartment, Nicky took the money out of his pocket. It was two twenty-dollar bills. He said, "Was he serious about me buying new clothes?"

"That guy's as serious as a heart attack," Frankie said. "And he's right. We'll go down to Venati's tomorrow and get you something more comfortable."

Nicky sat alone in his room that night, doodling and sketching his uncle and his uncle's goomba friends. He drew little portraits of Charlie Cement, and Sallie the Butcher, and Jimmy the Iceman, and Little Johnny Vegas.

Lying in bed, Nicky thought about Frankie and his friends—with "regular jobs." What if they were like the guys in *The Godfather*? "Sallie the Butcher" and "Jimmy the Iceman" were like names for contract killers. Charlie Cement could be the guy who buried the people they killed—in the river, with cement shoes. Oscar the Undertaker? Well, duh.

And his uncle? Obviously, he might be the boss. He might be the biggest goomba of them all. Nicky imagined Frankie facing down a line of cops. "You talking to me? You talking to *me*? 'Cause I'm the only one here. . . ."

Then he fell asleep.

CHAPTER FOUR

*V*enati's was a men's clothing store. The owner greeted Frankie like he was family and shook Nicky's hand.

"I knew your father," Venati said. "How come he don't come around here no more?"

"He had enough of mooks like you," Frankie said. "How about fixing my nephew up with some new duds? He needs something that's not so Banana Republic."

Venati picked out black jeans and black T-shirts, a pair of navy blue slacks and a light blue shirt with short sleeves and a little crown over the right pocket. Nicky thought it looked like a bowling shirt.

"Now he looks like a little goomba," Frankie said. "Not bad, eh?"

"Not bad," Nicky agreed.

They left Venati's side by side, one large goomba and one small goomba-in-training.

Back at the apartment, Grandma Tutti was rolling out dough. She said, "It's about time you're back. I need help with the macaroni. I'm making lasagna. Nicky, go wash your hands. You can cut."

For the next hour Nicky helped his grandmother make the noodles. She rolled the dough into big sheets. Nicky carved out strips three inches wide and twelve inches long. Grandma Tutti hung these on a rack "to dry," she said. By the time they were finished, strips of pale yellow noodles were hanging all over the apartment.

Around three o'clock Frankie came out of his room, carrying his gym bag and wearing black pants and a black leather jacket. He gave his mother a kiss and said, "See ya, Ma."

"You'll see me when?" Grandma Tutti asked.

"I'll see you when I get back," Frankie said. "You know how it is."

"I don't know anything," Grandma Tutti said. "You go out, you come back. It's a long time, it's a short time. How should I know when you're coming home?"

"Ma, if I knew, I'd tell you."

"Your father was the same way. He'd say he was going down to the corner for a pack of cigarettes and I wouldn't see him until the next morning."

"You shoulda made lasagna more often," Frankie said.

"*Out!*" Grandma Tutti said. "Out, you idiot!"

After Frankie had gone, Grandma Tutti brushed flour from her hands and said, "Okay. I'm going to make coffee and tell you something. Go sit in the other room and wait for me."

Nicky sat down in the room with the pictures of the Pope and Frank Sinatra and waited until his grandmother came down the hall with her coffee cup rattling in its saucer.

"Your mother called," Tutti said, and sat down across from him. "She says hello and she loves you and they're having a good time on the boat."

"It's actually a big ship, like a yacht."

"It's a ship. It's a yacht. It's a boat. The point is—school. She wants you to go to summer school."

"But that's for kids who are failing. I got straight As."

"That's not the problem," Grandma Tutti said. "It's your father. I didn't tell him Frankie was staying here.

Now he knows, and he thinks that, because of what Frankie does for a living, and who he hangs around with, he wants you to go home and live with Horace. Or Charlton."

"With *Clarence?*" Nicky was surprised. "But I like it here."

Nicky's grandmother smiled. "I told your father that," she said. "I told him you wouldn't be hanging around Frankie and his friends. I told him you were helping me. Then I told him you would go to summer school. In the end, he agreed."

Nicky said, "Okay. I guess. But what's the problem with Uncle Frankie and my dad, anyway?"

Tutti sighed and put down her coffee cup. "Your father was always jealous. Frankie was big and strong. He was good at sports. He was working with his father. Nicky stayed in his room and read books. Straight As he got—just like you. He thought his father was stupid. He thought his brother was stupid. He used to say, 'You don't know anything!'—like he was Albert Einstein himself."

"Wasn't his father proud of him, with the straight As?"

"Yes, and no," Tutti said. "He was very proud, secretly. But he was also a little ashamed that his son was so educated and he was so ignorant. So they fought. Nicky went away to Princeton. And he never came home—not for a weekend, or a holiday, not

Thanksgiving or Christmas. He wrote me letters. But he never came home once until his father died. He came home for the funeral. That's when he and your uncle Frankie fought. Nicky went back to Princeton and he and Frankie never made up."

Nicky said, "Wow. That's a long time to be angry."

"That's why your father is upset that your uncle is around. And that's why you're going to summer school."

"Okay," Nicky said. "When does it start?"

"School started yesterday," Grandma Tutti said. "You start in the morning."

The school was a wide two-story brick building, across the street from an enormous Catholic church with an asphalt playground next to it. Nicky arrived dressed in his Carrington school uniform of khaki slacks, white shirt and blue blazer. He followed his grandmother under an archway where I.S. 201 was carved in stone, down a hallway to a door that said "Attendance Office."

A grim woman who wore her eyeglasses on a chain pointed toward the end of the long linoleum hallway and said, "First period is math with Mr. Frommer, in room 220. It started five minutes ago. You're late."

Walking in late was awful. The students stared at

him. The teacher stared at him. As he was sitting down, one of the boys he'd seen on the street that first day called out, "Hey! It's the rich kid!" All the other kids laughed, and Nicky blushed.

Nicky watched the clock and drew in his sketch pad while Mr. Frommer droned on about area and volume. When the teacher asked, "Does anyone here remember the formula for finding the area of a rectangle?" Nicky reflexively raised his hand. The teacher said, "Yes, Richie?"

Nicky lowered his hand and put his face on the desk. The teacher called on someone else.

At the break, Nicky wasn't hungry. The other kids went to the cafeteria. He went to the schoolyard.

A group of boys was playing a game that involved a small red ball, about the size of a baseball. Nicky watched for a few minutes. Then the game stopped, and Nicky realized that the boys were all staring at him.

One of them, a blond kid with a turned-up nose, said, "Hey! You're standing on our field."

The kid next to him said, "So *move*."

The kid next to him said, "Make him move, Conrad."

Conrad dropped the ball, stepped forward and stuck his fists up.

Nicky gulped. This wasn't Carrington. This wasn't the grassy playing field of C-Prep. This was Brooklyn. So he stared at Conrad and said, "You talking to me?"

The kid said, *"What?"*

"Are you talking to *me?"*

"Of course I'm talking to you, you fruitcake."

" 'Cause I'm the only one here. Are you talking to—"

They were on him like *that*. The first kid pushed Nicky hard in the chest. A second kid swung his fist, and Nicky hit the ground and rolled. A kid was on his back, fists pummeling his shoulders. Then someone had him by his jacket collar and was lifting him up. Nicky closed his eyes and gritted his teeth against the punch he knew was coming.

Instead, a voice said, "Clear out, you brats—unless you want a piece of me."

Nicky opened his eyes. The guy holding his collar was another one of the kids he'd seen on the street his first day, the one his grandmother had called Tommy. He put Nicky on his feet and said, "You okay, or what?"

Nicky rubbed the gravel off his face. "Yeah."

"You sure?" Tommy grinned. "Those guys were going to give you a real beating. But they'll lay off now. They're just bullies, and bullies won't fight if they're afraid. Especially Conrad."

"Thanks for stepping in," Nicky said.

"*Fugheddaboudit.* I'm Tommy Caporelli. Howya doon?"

"I'm Nicholas Borelli. Nicky Borelli."

"I know that," Tommy said. "Frankie Borelli's nephew. What are you dressed for, your first communion? This is I.S. 201. We don't doll up for school here."

Tommy was wearing blue jeans and a T-shirt. He looked at his watch and said, "We still got time to get a Coke. Come on."

Nicky followed Tommy out the front gate and down the block to a little grocery store. Tommy led him to the candy aisle, where he draped an arm over Nicky's shoulder. He looked at the candy bars and took a long time deciding what he wanted. Finally he said, "Why don't you go and get a Coke?"

The man behind the cash register said, "One Coke? One dollar."

Tommy joined him at the counter. Nicky reached into his pocket and took out a dollar. He said, "You're not getting anything?"

"Nah. Let's blow."

Halfway back to the school gate, Tommy said, "Okay, stop." He stuck his hands into the pockets of Nicky's blazer and pulled out a Snickers bar, a Mars bar, a box of Milk Duds and a packet of Life Savers.

"You get first pick," he said.

Nicky said, "You *stole* all that?"

"*You* stole all that," Tommy said. "So whatta you want?"

"I'll take the Life Savers."

"Figures. Sissy." Tommy shoved the other candy into his pockets and said, "I'll see you after school."

Nicky was stunned. Tommy was a thief! Was he also a goomba? He'd ask Uncle Frankie about that when he got home.

Uncle Frankie didn't come home. But that night, while they were eating dinner, Nicky said, "I met a kid from the block, at school. Tommy Caporelli."

"He's a live one," Grandma Tutti said. "A good boy, but wild. Don't you let him get you into any trouble."

"What kind of trouble?"

"Who knows what kind of trouble, with boys like that? Just you watch your step and remember who you are."

"Who am I?"

"You're a Borelli. You're the son of Nicholas Borelli, the son of Arturo Borelli. Now help me with the dishes."

After dinner, Nicky watched goomba scenes from Frankie's DVD collection. One thing he noticed about the people in the movies: there were a lot of them. In *The Godfather*, or *Goodfellas*, or *Analyze This*, or *The So-*

pranos, no one was ever alone. If there was one goomba, there was a crowd of goombas.

Not for Nicky. He was mostly alone. He didn't see Tommy at school the next day. He sat in class, daydreaming and drawing faces in his sketch pad.

Especially in math. There was a dark-haired girl who sat by the blackboard. She was the prettiest girl Nicky had ever seen. While the teacher talked about equilateral and isosceles triangles, Nicky sketched her face from different angles. Whenever a student near him would raise a hand to answer a question, Nicky would close his sketch pad and pretend to be studying his textbook.

First period went by too quickly. Second period dragged.

The next day, Grandma Tutti sent Nicky to the bakery for fresh bread. He went around the corner, past the Bath Avenue Social Club. The door was ajar. Nicky peeked in. Eddie was making sandwiches behind the counter. Sallie the Butcher was playing cards with two men Nicky didn't recognize. He looked up, saw Nicky through the doorway and said, "Hey, Borelli! Come in here!"

Nicky went through the doorway. Sallie the Butcher stood up and said, "Guys, this is Nicky Borelli's boy— Frankie's nephew. What's going on?"

"I'm going to the bakery, for my grandmother."

"You're a good grandson. What's she cooking?"

"Something with clams."

"Linguini in clam sauce!" Sallie said. "Lucky kid! She cooks like an angel, your grandmother. I grew up on her ravioli."

"She's pretty good," Nicky said. "But she cooks too much. When Uncle Frankie's not around, we don't eat even half of it."

"Frankie's been working a lot, huh?"

"Yeah. All week."

"He's a hard worker, that Frankie."

"What about the other guys?" Nicky said. "Charlie, and Bobby, and all. Are they working, too?"

"Everybody except me. I go to work when everybody else is done." Sallie winked at the other two cardplayers. "I do my best work at night. Bada boom!"

That sealed it. Nicky was more certain than ever that his uncle and his crew were on some job. Maybe a big heist. Maybe armored cars. Or a bank. It must be a big job. All the men Nicky had met the first day in the social club must be on the job, too. And when they were done, Sallie the Butcher did his cutting.

And he *talked* about it, right out in the open. So the other two cardplayers must be part of the gang, too.

Nicky felt light-headed and strange. And a little scared. This was *so* not Carrington.

The old man who smelled funny was sitting on the front stoop—smoking a cigarette, but not sleeping—when Nicky came back. He grabbed Nicky's ankle in his bony hand and said, "Nicholas Borelli the Second! I am Vincente Moretti. Why did the chicken cross the road?"

Nicky said, "I don't know."

"To get the Chinese newspaper."

"I don't get it."

"Me neither," Mr. Moretti said. "I get the *New York Times*!"

Nicky smiled and said, "Now I get it."

Mr. Moretti tapped the ash off his cigarette and said, "Please tell your sainted grandmother that I am available for dinner this evening."

"Sure, Mr. Moretti. I'll tell her."

Upstairs, Nicky said, "That drunk guy on the stoop says he's available for dinner tonight."

"He can come to dinner—at my funeral," Grandma Tutti said. "Go wash up and we'll eat without him."

That night, after dinner, alone in his room, Nicky drew a comic strip of Frankie and his gang at work. They were in a sewer line, digging their way into a bank. Then they were in the bank, wiring explosives to the vault. They were in the vault, surrounded by money. But here came the cop cars! Frankie and his men took a stand in the alley behind the bank. The getaway car was coming! Bullets were flying!

There was a knock at the door. Nicky shoved his sketch pad under the bed.

"Good night, Nicky," his grandmother called to him. "I'll see you in the morning."

CHAPTER FIVE

$\mathcal{N}$icky had eaten his breakfast and was getting ready for school when Frankie came home.

He looked horrible. He needed a shave. His eyes were bloodshot. His clothes looked like he had slept in them. But when he saw Nicky, he lit up. He said, "Nicky Deuce in the house! C'mere, kid!" He pulled Nicky to his chest and gave him a big hug.

He smelled like he'd slept in his clothes, too. He let Nicky go, set down his gym bag with a clunk and said, "Come here, Ma. You give me a hug, too."

"Go wash first," Grandma Tutti said. "I know what you're like when you've been working."

"Some welcome home," Frankie said. "But I smell something good. What is that, Ma?"

"*Pasta e fagioli*, for later. Plus some fish."

"Pasta fazool!" Frankie said. "And fish! Tonight we'll eat like kings."

"Take a bath, Your Highness," Grandma Tutti said. "And you, get to school before you're late."

Nicky didn't see Tommy until math class, when his new friend came shuffling through the door, late, sat down behind Nicky and whispered, "Hey, hot dog. What'd I miss?"

Nicky smiled. "Not much."

"That's enough out of you, Caporelli," Frommer said. "Keep it down."

The lesson was all about measuring triangles. That was old news for Nicky. He opened his sketch pad and started drawing.

Frommer said, "To find the length of the longest side of a right triangle, we use the formula A squared plus B squared equals what, Mr. Caporelli?"

Tommy looked perplexed. He and Frommer stared at each other. Frommer turned back to the board. Nicky coughed the answer into his hand, loudly enough to be heard: "*C squared!*"

Frommer turned around and said, "Caporelli! You surprise me! A squared plus B squared always equals C squared, where C is the longest leg of a right triangle. Now, to find the area of a triangle . . ."

While Frommer wrote on the board, Nicky sketched him, transforming the teacher into a mad scientist with white hair and long fingernails.

Nicky was still drawing when Frommer turned and said, "Borelli? Problem five."

Nicky's textbook was inside his desk. Frommer was staring. The other students were staring. Nicky panicked. He felt like Sonny Corleone, in *The Godfather*, when he gets gunned down at the tollbooth.

"Borelli? That *is* your name, isn't it?"

Nicky said, "You talking to me?"

"Is your name Borelli or not?"

"Yeah. You got a problem with that?"

"I *beg* your pardon?"

"*Fugheddaboudit.*"

"Okay, smarty-pants—up! To the principal's office!"

It wasn't so bad. The principal was an elderly woman who reminded him of Grandma Tutti. She said, "If you're Nicholas Borelli, I think I knew your father. Wasn't he a student here in the seventies?"

"Yes, ma'am. And my uncle Frankie Borelli, too."

"Of course," the principal said. "I was a history teacher here then. Your father was an excellent student. And your uncle was an excellent, um, athlete. I have your records from Carrington Prep here. I see

49

you're following more in your father's tradition. So, can you explain your behavior in Mr. Frommer's classroom today?"

"No, ma'am. He called on me, and I sort of freaked out."

"Well, see that it doesn't happen again. Everyone knows and respects your uncle Frankie, but I can be very tough on troublemakers, and I'm happy to get tough on you if you're one of them. Now get on back to class."

Math was over. Tommy was in the yard. He ran over to Nicky and said, "That was awesome! Frommer almost had a heart attack. Next time he calls on me, I'm gonna say, 'You talking to *me*? Are you talking to *me*?' "

Nicky shook his head. "I gotta get a milk before the bell rings."

The cafeteria woman was just closing up. Nicky said, "Wait! Can I get a milk, please?"

The woman groaned but reached down for a milk.

"Two milks, please!"

Nicky turned. The dark-haired girl from first period ran up behind him. "Please!" she said.

Nicky leaned into the window and said, "Sorry. Could I have two milks, please?"

"Thanks," the girl said. "I'm Donna, by the way. We have math together. You're not from around here, huh?"

"No. I'm from New Jersey. Carrington."

"Wow. What are you doing *here*?"

"Staying with my grandmother."

"Too bad," Donna said. "I bet Carrington is nicer."

"It's okay. But the food is better here," Nicky said. "My grandma is a great cook. I get a lot of stuff I don't get at home. My mother is a vegetarian."

"That's funny," Donna said. "My dad's a butcher."

The bell rang. Donna said, "Gotta go! See you tomorrow in first period."

Tommy caught Nicky by the elbow just as Nicky was leaving school.

"By the way, thanks for saving me with Frommer today, before you got in trouble," he said.

Nicky coughed "C squared" into his hand and grinned. "*Fugheddaboudit.*"

Tommy laughed at him. "So what are you doing tomorrow night?"

"I don't know. Probably nothing."

"Excellent. I'll meet you right here, in front of school, at seven o'clock. We'll go do something."

"I'll see if I can."

"Cool. And what's the deal with you and that Donna, anyway?"

"Nothing. I just met her."

"Better not let Conrad see you. He's Donna's old boyfriend. He'll give you another beating."

"All I did was say hello to her."

"Forget it," Tommy said. "He won't touch you if he knows you know me. Plus he knows who your uncle is. If he forgets—remind him."

"Okay," Nicky said. "I'll see you tomorrow."

Grandma Tutti shushed Nicky when he got home and went into the kitchen.

"Your uncle Frank!" she whispered to him. "He's sleeping. He was up three nights straight. You can tell me everything later."

Later came. They could hear Uncle Frankie taking a shower. Nicky said, "So this guy from school asked me if I could hang out with him tomorrow night."

"What guy from school asked you that?"

"Tommy Caporelli."

Grandma Tutti clucked her tongue. "We'll ask your uncle."

When Uncle Frankie came out, he said, "Yo, Nicky," and gave his nephew a hug. He kissed his mother and said, "What's that smell?"

"We're having braciole and rigatoni," she said.

"Beautiful! Every guy needs a little *brajole*—eh, Nicky?" He winked at his nephew. "So how's it going over at the school?"

"He's got a date to go make trouble with Tommy Caporelli tomorrow."

"Saturday night with the boys," Frankie said. "That's good. But with most guys it's *Friday* night out with the boys, and the *goomars*. Saturday night is for the families and the wives."

Nicky said, "What's a *goomar*?"

"It's, you know, a girlfriend. Or a mistress."

"Frankie!" Grandma Tutti said. "Are you teaching him to be a jerk?"

"Ma, I'm just telling him how it is," Frankie said. "And don't worry about Tommy Caporelli. He's a little wild, maybe. But that's okay. My friends, when they were kids, they were *all* wild. And they're still my best friends today."

"Sit down and have some dinner," Grandma Tutti said.

At the table, Frankie said, "I remember Charlie Cement figured out a way to get free food from Fat Farouk—you remember him, right?"

Nicky nodded. "The hot dog guy?"

"Right. One of us would ask Fat Farouk for a cream soda. Then he'd pay for it, all in nickels and pennies. While he was doing that, another kid would let the air out of one of Fat Farouk's tires. Then the first kid would say, 'Hey, Fat Farouk! You got a flat tire!' Farouk would go look, and a third kid would grab a handful of hot dogs and buns. We'd have a feast."

"Frankie!" his mother chided. "That's a terrible story."

"Then, the best part," Frankie said. "Two other guys

53

would come along a few minutes later and offer to fix his tire for a dollar."

"Would he pay you?"

"Of course. What's he gonna do? He's so fat, he can't change his own shoes without help."

"Frankie!" his mother said.

"It's true," Frankie said. "I found out later that Fat Farouk knew what was going on the whole time. He was friends with Charlie Cement's dad. He'd go visit him and say, 'You owe me five bucks for hot dogs your kid stole.' And Charlie's dad would pay up. Some hoodlums we were!"

"Those were bad boys, your friends," Tutti said.

"It wasn't just them," Frankie said. "Your goody-goody son Nicky found a way to get free soda. You remember those old-fashioned soda machines with the bottles lined up behind a glass door? Nicky carried a bottle opener in his pocket, and a straw. When he'd get thirsty, we'd go over to the gas station. He'd open that glass window, pick out a flavor, pop the cap and stick the straw in. He'd drink it down, then pass the opener and the straw to the next guy. Free soda!"

Grandma Tutti said, "Hooligans!"

"We had a ball," Frankie said. "I wish it never ended."

Nicky said, "It's hard to imagine my dad doing that stuff."

"I know," Frankie said. "It didn't last. He got serious

about school and all. Then he grew up! The rest of us are still acting like kids."

"You can say that again," Grandma Tutti said. "You and your friends. You're still a bunch of hoodlums."

"That's right, Ma," Frankie said. "Speaking of growing up, Salvatore Carmenza's getting married again."

"Already?" Tutti said. "His first wife is barely cold in the ground."

"Ma! Eight years!"

"He's rushing into it," Tutti said. "Who's the new wife? And where is the wedding taking place?"

"Carol Grimaldi. And Scarantino's. The wedding hall."

"Expensive," Grandma Tutti said. "The *a boost* is going to kill you."

"Tell me about it," Frankie said.

Nicky said, "What's a *boost*?"

"The *a boost*," Frankie said. "It's the money you give people at a wedding. Or a funeral. Or a first communion, or maybe a birthday party. It's just a little money to help with the expenses."

"How much is it?" Nicky asked.

"It depends. With a place like Scarantino's, and the food they serve, and the cost of the band, the *a boost* will have to be three or four *hunge*."

"Three or four *hundred*?"

"At least. But what are you gonna do? He's my best

friend since grade school, and I'm the best man. Can I give a crummy *a boost*? I'd never hear the end of it."

After dinner, Frankie and Nicky stretched out in the family room. Frankie cranked the easy chair out until it was almost level with the floor, and he let out a huge sigh.

"It's good to be home," he said. "It's good to have you here, too. You hear anything else from your folks?"

"Not since they called and made me go to school."

"That's good, though, right? You made a friend already."

"Yeah. I guess so."

"Otherwise, you'd be hanging around with your grandma all day. That's not much fun."

"Why isn't it?" Grandma Tutti asked as she came into the room. "We have fun, Nicky and me."

"I bet you have a ball when I'm not here," Frankie said. "Speaking of which, I have to go away again. I gotta see a guy in Arizona."

"Arizona! In the summer! Who goes to Arizona in the summer?"

"Me, Ma. I leave in the morning. I should be back on Sunday night."

"But, Frankie!" his mother said. "You know what day tomorrow is."

"I know, Ma, believe me. But you got Nicky. He can go with you."

Nicky said, "Go where?" But no one answered him.

Frankie checked his watch and said, "That's settled. Now we can have some entertainment. They got *Scarface* on TV—the original, with Paul Muni, not the Cuban one with Al Pacino. So everybody don't talk for a while."

Fifteen minutes later, before Scarface had pulled his first caper, Frankie was snoring in his easy chair. Grandma Tutti said, "Listen to him. Like an ox. You turn the TV off when you're done, okay?"

She gave Nicky a kiss on the forehead and said, "Good night."

When the movie ended, Nicky turned the TV off, left his snoring uncle and went down the hallway. Frankie's door was open. His gym bag lay on the floor next to the bed.

Nicky knelt down and unzipped the bag.

It was an armory. There were three pistols. There were a dozen ammunition clips. There were two things that looked like safety flares, and two things that looked like hand grenades. Lying next to the bag was a bullet-proof vest.

Nicky went down the hall to his room fast and shut his bedroom door.

Whatever his uncle was doing was serious. Why did he need all those weapons? You didn't go someplace with that kind of firepower if you were just kidding around. This was war. And the guys Uncle Frankie was fighting—did they have weapons like that, too? Was that why he had a bulletproof vest? What if he got shot?

Maybe that was why he was going to Arizona. Maybe he was on the lam. Maybe he was going to lie low for a few days, until the heat was off. Maybe he would be okay.

Nicky went to bed. He had trouble falling asleep. He tried to imagine Uncle Frankie in Phoenix, at a swanky hotel, by the pool, or playing golf, underneath a palm tree, or a cactus. He tried to imagine Uncle Frankie safe. He fell asleep still trying.

CHAPTER SIX

$\mathcal{U}$ncle Frankie had gone when Nicky got up. Grandma Tutti was in the kitchen, humming a song to herself. She turned and said, "Come and have some breakfast. We're going to the cemetery."

"What for?"

"It's my wedding anniversary today. I always go visit your grandfather on our anniversary. Sit down and eat, and we'll go."

It took almost an hour to get there. First they walked to the corner, Nicky's grandmother carrying a shoulder bag and a bouquet of fresh flowers. They caught a bus, took another bus, walked for several blocks, took another bus and finally walked through the gates of a cemetery spread out over a rolling green hill.

"Look around," his grandmother said when they got near the top of the hill. "These are your people."

There were half a dozen Borellis. Nearby there were Capotortos and Bolinos and Ventimiglias and Fiandras and a hundred other Italian families. Nicky's grandmother opened her shoulder bag. Out came a tablecloth, some sandwiches wrapped in wax paper, a bottle of Pellegrino water, two apples and a camera.

While they ate, Grandma Tutti pointed at the headstones.

"Mrs. Bolino did my hair the day I got married," she said. "She had a little shop. The Fiandras had a fruit store. Carmine Potenza—I remember his funeral like it was yesterday—was your grandfather's partner in the brick business. You see the big monument there, with the flying angel?"

Nicky looked and nodded.

"That is the Faronellis'. Mr. Faronelli was the *patrone*. Very powerful man—and rich. Very kind. When your uncle Frankie broke his foot, Mr. Faronelli sent someone to speak with the company that was delivering the bricks. All that time in the hospital for your uncle, and your grandfather and I never saw a bill. That's how problems were solved in the old days. Now let's take a picture."

Grandma Tutti began patting her hair and straightening her dress. She stood in the empty space next to her husband's headstone—the empty space where, Nicky realized, Grandma Tutti would be one day. She rested her hand gently on the stone and said, "Like this. Get the camera."

Nicky said, "You want me to take a picture?"

"No. I want you to take an X ray. Of course take a picture. Just like this."

Nicky held the camera so that his grandmother was in the center of the frame, next to her husband's grave.

"No," she said. "Make sure your grandfather is in the picture. Can you read the writing?"

Nicky moved closer until he could read "Arturo Borelli. Requiescat in Pace. 1912–1977." He could see all of his grandmother but her feet.

"Yes."

"Take the picture."

The camera clicked. Tutti said, "Okay. Take some more, to make sure."

"Do you want to stand on the other side or something?"

Grandma Tutti said, "Nicky, no. *This* is my place. On this side. We slept in the bed that way, too. Take some more pictures, and we can go home."

* * *

Tommy was waiting for him that night in front of the school. He called, "Yo, Nicky!" and waved. Nicky almost laughed out loud. *"Yo, Nicky!"* Nobody had ever called out to him like that before. He liked it.

"What's up?" he asked.

"We gotta go see this guy," Tommy said. "We got a chance to make a couple of bucks. Then we can go to the movies or something."

"Make a couple of bucks how?"

"I dunno. We gotta check it out."

They took off running. Tommy led him down one street, over a block, through an alley, across a park, down another street, through the front door of a deli and out the back door onto a different street.

Nicky, out of breath, said, "This is like playing *SimCity*."

"More like *Grand Theft Auto*," Tommy said. "That's the best."

"Maybe the best street game," Nicky agreed. "But *BlackPlanet* is the best."

Tommy said, "You're right. *BlackPlanet* is genius."

Nicky stopped dead. "Whoa. You play *BlackPlanet*?"

"Who doesn't?" Tommy said.

Nicky beamed. "What level?"

"I'm in nine—almost ten. What about you?"

Nicky said, "I haven't even beaten eight. You must have all the cheats."

"C'mon, man. I've *invented* cheats. This is it."

Tommy led Nicky through the front door of a corner candy store. There was a little old man behind the counter. He jerked his head toward the rear of the store and said, "Over there."

A man wearing an overcoat and a baseball cap—in summer, on a warm evening—was sitting in the back. He looked at the two boys over the rim of his coffee cup and said, "Siddown. You're Tommy, right?"

"That's right," Tommy said.

"You're supposed to be alone."

"This is Nicky. He's okay."

"Siddown—both of youse."

The man had yellow skin, and he smelled like cigarettes. When he smiled, his teeth were yellow, too.

"Here's the deal," he said. "You don't know me. We never met. You never saw me. Got that?"

Tommy nodded and poked Nicky. Nicky nodded, too.

"If you forget that, you're finished. *Capeesh?*"

The man took an envelope out of his overcoat pocket, withdrew five twenty-dollar bills and spread them on the table in front of him. The bills looked greasy and old. Nicky thought at once of his uncle and the counterfeit twenties his friends used to pass.

"This is a hundred dollars," the yellow man said. "Alls you got to do is spend it. You can buy whatever you want with it. There's only two things you got to remember. One, never spend two bills in the same place. Two, never buy anything that costs more than ten bucks. Got that?"

Tommy nodded and said, "Why?"

"Because I said so," the yellow man said, and raised one yellow hand like he was going to smack Tommy. But Tommy didn't flinch. The man smiled. He said, "Tough guy, huh? That's the deal. Spend these bills. Buy whatever you want. Bring me the change. You get a hundred bucks, and you bring back fifty. You keep half. I get half. Got that?"

Tommy smiled and said, "Sure. It's easy."

"What about you?" the man said to Nicky.

"Sure," Nicky said. "You're making us an offer we can't refuse."

Tommy turned and stared at him. The man with the yellow skin stared, too. Then he said, "Just spend the money, and bring me back half. Keep your mouth shut. If anyone looks at you sideways, run like hell. And whatever happens, you never, ever say nothing about me. If you do—right?—you're cooked."

"Great," Tommy said, and shoved the bills into his pocket.

"Come back here exactly a week from now, and you'll get a hundred bucks more," the man said.

Out on the street, Tommy took Nicky's arm and pulled him halfway down the block before he spoke.

"Can you believe this? Fifty bucks—for nothing!"

"Sweet," Nicky said. "I guess."

"You guess what? It's beautiful. Couldn't you use fifty bucks?"

"I don't know. I have some money already."

"Yeah, me too. About fifty *cents*." Tommy took the twenties out of his pocket and waved them in Nicky's face. "Hey, what if we took the whole hundred and never went back?"

"Don't you think that guy would come and get us?"

"That guy? Give me a break!" Tommy thought about it. "Well, maybe. Come on. Let's see if this thing works. I'll let you go first."

"Why me?"

"Because I said so. Here."

They stopped in front of a corner grocery store. Tommy said, "Go on. Buy me a Mars bar."

Nicky went into the store, the greasy twenty clutched in his sweaty hand. A man was sitting behind the counter, reading *Daily Racing Form*. He didn't even look up. Nicky came back with a Mars bar and a roll of Life Savers.

The man glanced at the candy, said, "A dollar sixty, out of twenty," and counted out a ten, a five, three ones and forty cents in change.

Nicky said, "Thanks," and went outside.

Tommy wasn't there. Nicky held the change in his

pocket, his head light, his heart pounding in his chest, and looked up and down the block. No Tommy. Nicky started walking toward the corner. Tommy stepped out of the shadows between two buildings.

"So? How'd it go?"

Nicky jumped. "What are you doing?"

"I was being your lookout," Tommy said. "How'd it go? Did it work?"

"It worked fine." Nicky handed him the Mars bar and the change.

Tommy said, "Beautiful!" and stuck the money in his pocket. "Let's go over a few blocks and try it again. Then we can go to a movie. We use a twenty to buy tickets. Then we use another twenty each to buy some popcorn or something. That's five twenties. We'll have fifty bucks in, like, less than an hour!"

They passed the next twenty at a deli. Nicky went in, bought two Cokes and got eighteen dollars in change. He and Tommy drank the sodas while they walked across town to the movie theater. The streets were busy. There were couples walking hand in hand, and groups of girls and boys walking together or standing around on stoops.

Two policemen stood talking on the corner. Nicky got nervous. What if there was a report about two boys passing counterfeit twenties? Would they be able to identify Nicky and Tommy? No. Just Nicky. He imagined the cops turning and shouting, "There he is!" He imagined running. The cops would shout, "Stop, in the name of the law!" or, "Stop, or I'll shoot!"

By the time they got to the corner, Nicky was trembling with fear. Tommy nodded at the policemen. "Howzit going?"

One cop turned and said, "Hiya, kid."

Nicky almost fainted.

A few blocks on, Tommy said, "It's over here." When they turned the corner, Nicky could see the marquee. It was all movies that he'd already seen. Tommy said, "Hey! They got *Summer of the Living Night*."

Inside, Nicky slumped in his seat and watched the coming attractions without seeing. He was thinking about jails, and prisons, and the guy his uncle knew who went to prison and got shot to death in a robbery.

When the feature started, Tommy leaned over and said, "Who said crime doesn't pay? Fifty bucks in one hour! I'm saving up for *BlackPlanet Two*."

"It's supposed to come out soon, right?" Nicky asked.

"For Christmas," Tommy said confidently.

After the movie, Tommy and Nicky walked back to Bath Avenue. When they got to Nicky's street, Tommy said, "You're all right, Nicky. I wasn't sure, you being from Jersey and all. I thought you might chicken out."

"I didn't chicken out. I went first."

"You did good. And now you got twenty-five bucks

to buy anything you want. We'll go back next week, and he'll give us another hundred, and we can make another fifty, right?"

"Right," Nicky said, faint at the idea of having to go through all that again.

Tommy said, "You going to church in the morning?"

"Church? I don't think so," Nicky said.

"C'mon. With *your* grandmother? You know she's going. I'll see you there."

Tommy stuck a hand out, and they shook. Nicky said, "See ya," and turned and ran down the block to his grandmother's apartment.

CHAPTER SEVEN

$\mathcal{N}$icky's grandmother woke him early the next morning. He checked the clock as she was leaving the room—seven-fifteen?—and jumped out of bed. He was halfway down the hall when he remembered it was Sunday.

His grandmother was drinking coffee in the kitchen. Nicky kissed her on the cheek and said, "Why are we up so early?"

"It's Sunday."

"That's what I mean," Nicky said. "Why are we up so early on Sunday?"

"Because we're going to eight o'clock mass and we're

not going to be late. Go get your school clothes on and brush your teeth. And your hair."

There were three old women waiting outside, cackling like birds, when Nicky and his grandmother went down the steps.

"This is my grandson, Nicky," Tutti said.

"Good morning, Nicky," the old birds sang.

"This is Mrs. Mascali, Mrs. Vitta and Mrs. Mazzone," Grandma Tutti said. "Come on. We're late already."

The four women gossiped all the way to church. Nicky trailed behind. At the corner, he heard a voice whisper, "Hey, Borelli!" He turned. Tommy was grinning at him.

"Hey, you crook," Tommy said. "What's going on?"

"Church with Grandma," Nicky said.

"Told you so," Tommy said. "My mom's already there. She goes to the seven o'clock mass, and then gives me a beatin' if I don't show up for the eight o'clock."

"You talk nice about your mother, Tomasino Caporelli," Grandma Tutti said. "And don't think I can't hear you."

"Good morning, Mrs. Borelli," Tommy said.

Nicky leaned toward Tommy and said, "Tomasino? Your real name is *Tomasino?*"

"Make something out of it, and I'll kick you to the curb."

He dashed off and disappeared.

Nicky had never been to regular mass. His parents sometimes went to a service at Christmas, or before a wedding, and almost always to the bright new Carrington Catholic Church, between the Carrington Country Club and Carrington Galleria.

This was different. This was St. Peter's, and it was like a cathedral. It was dark inside, and cool, and smelled like it was a thousand years old. Light streamed in through the dark blue stained glass. Jesus hung from every wall, crowned in thorns and agony. A pipe organ played from somewhere. Nicky's grandmother led him to a long wooden bench and they sat with her elderly friends.

Three rows forward, and over to the left, Nicky saw Donna. She was sitting with a woman wearing a hat. Donna whispered something to the woman, and the woman turned and stared at Nicky. Grandma Tutti waved, and the woman waved back.

Nicky said, "Who's that lady?"

"That's Carol Grimaldi," Tutti said, "the one who's marrying Salvatore Carmenza. Sallie the Butcher, they call him."

Nicky was stunned. His grandmother knew that Salvatore Carmenza was called Sallie the Butcher? Did she know what that meant? Was she in on the whole thing? Nicky's head spun. Was she some sort of mobster grandma, like Tony Soprano's mother, Livia? It didn't seem possible.

The service lasted about a week, even though it only took an hour. Nicky sat on the hard bench, wondering whether everyone in the room was as uncomfortable as he was. He tried not to stare at Donna the whole time—and failed.

Nicky followed his grandmother to the front of the church when it was all over. She stopped to say thank you to the priest. "This is my grandson, Nicholas," she said. "Nicky, say hello to Father Michael."

"Hello, Father."

Outside, Tommy was standing with some kids Nicky recognized from his first day in Bensonhurst. Because Tommy was there, he went over to them.

"Hey," he said.

The group turned to him.

One boy said, "Hey. It's the rich kid again."

"How's it going, Richie Rich?"

"Hey, Tommy," Nicky called out.

"Yeah. Hey."

Nicky said, "You guys playing ball today?"

The first kid said, "Sure, Richie Rich. Bring your pom-poms. We need a cheerleader."

The other kids laughed—all except Tommy. He stared at the ground.

Nicky said, "Very funny. I've seen you guys play, though. Not much to cheer about."

"Yo!" the first kid said. "Mr. Preppy-Prep has a smart mouth!" The kid stepped forward and gave Nicky a shove in the chest. "You looking for some trouble?"

Nicky stumbled back a step and said, "No."

"I think you are." The kid gave Nicky another shove.

Tommy stepped up and said, "Stop it, Gene." He put his hand on the kid's shoulder. "Nicky's okay."

"You know this guy?" Gene said.

"Yeah. He's okay," Tommy said.

"Then I won't kill him—*today*," Gene said. "Let's get outta here."

Tommy followed Gene and the other kids. Nicky, his stomach sick and his face red, walked back over to his grandmother.

"What's wrong?" she asked. "You look terrible."

"I'm just hungry, is all."

"Come," Tutti said. "We'll stop at Capaldi's on the way home, and then you can have breakfast."

Tutti led the way again, with her three ancient pals. "We're going to Capaldi's," she said to the ladies. "Come and have coffee at noon. I'll buy a little cake."

Capaldi's was a bakery on the next block. Despite the early hour, there was a line of women waiting outside.

"It's always busy on Sunday morning," Tutti

explained. "Mr. Capaldi bakes on Saturday night. He's the only one who has fresh pastries on a Sunday morning. You can get a bear claw or a cannoli or something."

Capaldi himself was standing inside, dressed in a beautifully tailored suit and fine Italian shoes.

Nicky said, "How come he's all dressed up?"

"He likes to look nice," Grandma Tutti said.

"Is he so rich, from being a baker?"

"He has a little side business," Grandma Tutti said. "But no one talks about it."

Back at the apartment, Tutti said, "You get changed and come help me in the kitchen while we eat breakfast. I'm making eggplant parmigiana and a chicken."

Tutti was reading the paper when Nicky came back dressed in his jeans and T-shirt. She clucked her tongue and said, "Augusto Perontino. Dead. He and I were exactly the same age. So handsome! I used to think if I hadn't met your grandfather—well!"

The picture in the paper showed a dapper man in an overcoat and a fedora. He was seventy-four. He was survived by about six hundred people.

"He had a lot of children, and a *lot* of grandchildren," Nicky said. "Fifteen grandchildren. Six great-grandchildren."

"He was a lucky man," Tutti said. "Me, with two

sons, I have only one grandchild. You better hurry, if I'm going to have any great-grandchildren. Maybe you and that Donna, eh?"

Nicky stared at his grandmother.

"What?" she said. "Don't I have eyes in my head? I saw you, in church."

After breakfast, Nicky took the newspaper into the family room. It was the same news they got in Carrington. The president. The economy. The ball games. And lots of crimes. Nicky liked reading about the crimes. He looked for stories that had something to do with Bensonhurst. There weren't any. Until the next to the last page.

Under the headline "Cops Foil Payroll Robbery," there was a story about a heist gone wrong. Undercover police officers, acting on an informant's tip, had staked out a meatpacking firm on Bayshore. Heavily armed thieves overpowered the firm's security staff early Saturday and escaped with more than $150,000 in payroll money. The undercover officers gave chase. One of the thieves was killed in the ensuing gun battle. One was taken into custody. Three men escaped. Police recovered all the payroll money.

There were no pictures. Nicky didn't need any. He could easily imagine his uncle Frankie lying dead on the floor of some rancid meatpacking plant, or arrested by plainclothes police officers while Charlie Cement or Oscar the Undertaker lay bleeding to death at his feet. Which three escaped? Was Frankie one of them?

For the first time in his life, Nicky closed his eyes and prayed. "Please don't let anything bad happen to Uncle Frankie. Amen."

Grandma Tutti's old-lady pals were starting to arrive. Nicky kissed his grandmother goodbye and said, "I'm going out to play for a while."

Mr. Moretti was sitting on the stoop. Nicky tried to skip by, but the old man caught him by the ankle and said, "Nicholas Borelli the Second! Stop! Do you know where they put the noisy dog?"

"No, sir."

"In the *barking* lot. Do you know why the pony had a sore throat?"

"No, sir."

"He was a little *horse*. Do you know how many Italians—"

"Excuse me, Mr. Moretti. I have to go."

Tommy and a group of boys Nicky didn't recognize were playing stickball on the corner. Nicky wandered up slowly. He didn't want to appear too eager. He didn't want to play, even. He wasn't very good at sports. But he didn't want to be left out, either.

When Tommy saw Nicky, he said, "Yo! Here's our outfield. C'mere."

Nicky jogged over. Tommy said, "Guys, this is Nicky. He's Frankie Borelli's nephew. Don't screw around with him, or you're dead, right?"

A couple of the kids laughed nervously.

"All right," Tommy said. "Nicky, you're outfield. Anything comes your way, catch it in the air. If you can't catch it in the air, throw it to first base. You gotta throw it to the base to get the batter out. Got it?"

Nicky took up a position in the middle of the street, about twenty feet behind the guy playing second base. Tommy was the pitcher. Two other kids stood next to parked cars that were supposed to be first base and third base. A kid with bright red hair was the batter. He swung a short length of broomstick like he was going to chop the ball to bits.

Then Nicky noticed Nutty. He was dressed up like an umpire, with the striped shirt, the black pants and a baseball cap. He even had a whistle, which he blew at intervals that had nothing to do with the ball game.

Tommy said, "All right. Batter up." He bounced the ball toward the plate. The redheaded kid smacked at it with the broomstick and missed. Tommy cackled at him and said, "Strike one." He bounced the ball again. This time the redheaded kid sent the ball sailing toward third base—and right through the open window of a parked Cadillac.

The second baseman turned to Nicky and said, "Oh, man. That's Little Johnny Vegas' Cadillac."

Nutty blew his whistle. Tommy said, "Inside a parked car doesn't count. You can play it over."

The redhead got a hit. Tommy caught the ball and made an out, and it was his team's turn to hit. When he got up to bat, Tommy smacked a ball straight down the middle of the street. Tommy rounded the bases like he had won the World Series. The next batter got out, and Tommy's team returned to the field.

The redhead took his position at the plate again. Tommy bounced the ball toward him and got a strike. The redhead swung hard at the next ball, and it shot off the broomstick, straight over Tommy's head, and straight toward Nicky.

He didn't panic. He stuck his hands up. He took two quick steps backward. The ball was getting close. It was moving *really* fast. Nicky took two more steps back. A car horn sounded. The ball was in his hands. Everything went black.

Nicky woke up slowly. He heard voices. His eyes swam. He was staring at the sky. Nutty was looking down at him. A voice off to the side was saying, "He just kept coming! I was stopped! You saw I was stopped!"

Then Tommy was kneeling beside him. He said, "You okay, Nicky?"

"Yeah."

"Are you sure?"

"Yeah." Nicky felt his hands. The ball was still there. "Did I get him out?"

"Listen to this guy!" Tommy said. "What an athlete!"

Tommy helped him to his feet. Nicky's legs felt rubbery. He dropped the ball and wobbled a little. Tommy held his arm until he could stand right. Nicky said, "Maybe I shouldn't play anymore."

"No kidding," Tommy said. "I'll walk you home."

The redhead, when Nicky passed, said, "Nice catch, man."

Tommy rang the bell and pushed open the door of Grandma Tutti's apartment. Nicky went up the stairs, unsteady, with his friend behind him. In the kitchen, Nicky's grandmother and her old-lady friends were sitting with their coffee and cake. Tutti stood up and said, "Here's my grandson," and then rushed to his side. "For God's sake, what happened?"

"He's okay," Tommy said. "He had a little accident."

"An accident! Tommy Caporelli, if I find out you've hurt my grandson, I'll—"

"It's not like that," Nicky said. "We were playing ball and I ran into a car."

"Come and sit. Maria! Get some ice. Where does it hurt?"

The old women fussed over him. Tommy gave Nicky a big wink and then was gone. Someone got Nicky a

79

glass of milk and a plate of cookies. The ice pack went on his head. He kept saying, "I'm fine, honest." The old women chattered in Italian.

Fifteen minutes later, the bell rang. Grandma Tutti sent one of the other ladies to the door. Nicky heard the voice from the street again.

"I was stopped! He kept coming backwards! Mrs. Borelli, you have to believe me!"

"You gotta tell Frankie I didn't do nothing," the man said. "The car was stopped! I didn't even know the kid was your grandson!"

"It's all right, Angelo," Grandma Tutti told him. "The boy's fine."

"I hardly touched him! But you gotta tell Frankie it wasn't my fault."

"All right, already," Grandma Tutti said. "Out!"

Dinner was delicious. After the events of the day, though—church, the shove he'd gotten from Gene, the scary news story about the payroll robbery, the heroic stickball catch and then the automobile accident— Nicky had no appetite. He nibbled. He could feel his grandmother watching him. She said to him, "You look sad. Do you miss your parents?"

He felt too tired to explain himself. So he said, "Yeah. I guess so."

After Nicky had taken the trash can out to the curb,

and his grandmother had done the dishes, she said, "I picked up our pictures from the cemetery. Go get the big red photo album from the den."

Grandma Tutti had the pictures out when he got back. She said, "Which is the best one?"

To Nicky they looked identical. He pointed at one—his grandmother standing next to her husband's grave, her hand resting lightly on the headstone—and said, "I like this one."

"That one is good," she said, and flopped the photo album open to the first empty page. There was already one picture pasted in. As his grandmother started fitting in the new one, Nicky saw that the old one was exactly the same shot: his grandmother, dressed in her best Sunday black, standing next to the grave of her husband.

He turned the pages. The entire photo album was filled with pictures of his grandmother standing next to her husband's grave. Every picture was the same. Grandma on the left. Grandpa's headstone on the right.

"Thank God you were here," Tutti said. "Otherwise it might have been the first time in twenty-seven years that I didn't get a picture on my anniversary. It's a blessing having you around."

She kissed her grandson on the head.

"And it's not so bad for you, either," she said. "One

week here, and you've already got a best friend, and a girlfriend, and you're a sports hero!"

That night, Nicky sat in bed with his sketch pad, looking over the drawings he'd done already. There were sketches of his grandmother and his uncle Frankie, plus some of Donna. There were cartoony drawings of Tommy, and a scary picture of the yellow man. On one page were several drawings of Nutty—as a cop, as a baseball umpire, as a pilot.

His grandmother was right, Nicky thought: it was a lot for one week. And she didn't even know the part about the counterfeit twenties.

CHAPTER EIGHT

Frankie was home. Sitting in his room, Nicky heard the front door open and felt the heavy weight of his uncle's steps coming down the hall. But when he went to Frankie's room to say hello, the door was closed.

At dinner, Frankie didn't talk much. Grandma Tutti told him the story of Nicky's accident and made fun of the trembling Angelo. Frankie hardly smiled. After the meal, Nicky wanted to ask his uncle to take him to the Bath Avenue Social Club, to see if the guys were all okay, but Frankie didn't even suggest going out for an ice cream. Instead Frankie went out without saying where he was going or when he was coming back.

That night there was a call from Nicky's mother. The cruise was a big success. They were having fun. Nicky's father was getting along very well with his boss—so well that the boss had invited Nicky's parents to join him at his summer house in St. Barts. "They're skeet shooting today!" she said.

"Dad is *skeet* shooting?" Nicky asked. "Are you serious?"

"Apparently he's very good," his mother said. "Yesterday he hit two, uh, skeets. Also, here's some good news. The camp is reopening. You can still go!"

Nicky thought about Noah and Chad and Jordan, and Camp Wannameka, and swimming and rowing. Then he thought about Uncle Frankie, Tommy, Donna, his grandmother's cooking, his uncle's gang, the man with the yellow skin, the twenty-dollar bills . . .

"What's the matter?" his mother asked.

"Nothing," Nicky answered. "It's great. I can't wait."

"Try to be patient," she said. "Now let me talk to your grandmother again."

His mother and his grandmother made the deal. Nicky would stay another week. Then he'd be shipped off to Camp Wannameka.

Grandma Tutti said, "Or he could stay here an extra week, if he wants."

Then she added, "Of course it's up to you."

After school the next day, Tommy grabbed Nicky's arm and said, "So, what are you doing tonight? You wanna hang out?"

"Sure," Nicky said.

"Come get me around six," Tommy said. "It's right around the corner—717 Cropsey Avenue. First floor."

Nicky told his grandmother he was going to spend the evening with Tommy Caporelli. She frowned, but said, "As long as your uncle says it's okay."

"Is he here?"

"No," Tutti said. "He's up the street, at the club. Go and ask him."

Nicky dashed to the Bath Avenue Social Club. Inside, his uncle was deep in conversation with Sallie the Butcher, Jimmy the Iceman, Oscar the Undertaker and Charlie Cement, studying some papers laid out on the table.

Frankie looked up and said, "Hey! It's Nicky Deuce, the stickball terror of Bath Avenue."

Sallie the Butcher swept the papers into a pile and put them in a briefcase as Nicky approached the table. He stood up and said to Frankie, "We'll finish talking about this later, huh?"

"Sure," Frankie said. "But we need blueprints. I've cased the joint, but it's been a couple of years. We need to know about the exits and entrances, and how the crew gets in and out."

"I know a guy who knows a guy," Charlie said. "I'll take care of that."

"Sit, Nicky!" Frankie said. "Eddie! Get him a sandwich."

Between bites, Nicky said, "Grandma says to ask you if I can hang out with Tommy Caporelli tonight."

"What are you guys gonna do?" Frankie asked.

"I don't know," Nicky said. "A movie or something."

"Sounds good," Frankie said. "C'mere." He pulled a bankroll out of his pants pocket and peeled off a twenty. "Don't stay out too late."

Nicky hit the street running, then ran back in and said, "Thanks for the sandwich, Eddie," and ran back out again. He was a block away before he realized he hadn't even told his uncle about the phone call from his mother.

Tommy's apartment was ten or twelve blocks from Grandma Tutti's. It wasn't that far away, but it was *different*. The houses looked older. The railings and fences needed paint. When Nicky rang the doorbell at 717 Cropsey, nothing happened. He waited half a minute, then knocked.

Tommy came sprinting down the stairs and said, "Hey. C'mon in."

The apartment was dark, and it smelled like cooking oil and mildew. The wallpaper was peeling in the hallway, which led to a living room filled with worn furniture. Tommy said, "Come on out back," and led Nicky through the kitchen. A man was sitting at a linoleum table, wearing a sleeveless T-shirt and smoking a cigarette. He looked up from the newspaper and said, "Who's this?"

"My friend Nicky," Tommy said.

"You guys wanna watch some TV?"

"Maybe later, Harvey."

The man grunted and went back to his paper.

There were two ruined lounge chairs sitting beside a weedy-looking garden.

"My grandpa's garden," Tommy said. "He grows tomatoes and *gagoots*. I hate *gagoots*."

"What's *gagoots*?"

"Squash," Tommy said. "Whatta you call it—zucchini."

"I like zucchini," Nicky said. "You can make ratatouille."

"*You* can make ratatouille," Tommy said. "I don't eat any of that Mexican junk."

"Was that your grandpa reading the paper?"

"That was Harvey," Tommy said. "My mother's boyfriend."

"Does he live here?"

"Sometimes," Tommy said. "He comes, he stays, he leaves—it depends on if my mother's working."

"Why?"

" 'Cause most of the time she works two jobs, which means there's no one around to look after Gramps when I'm at school," Tommy said. "You want a Coke?"

"Sure."

Tommy went back inside the house. Nicky heard the refrigerator door open, then shut. Tommy came back.

"No Cokes," he said. "But check out that smell."

Nicky sniffed the air. "Somebody's grilling."

The two boys went to the fence at the back of the yard and stared through the slats. A man wearing nothing but a Speedo bathing suit was standing over a Weber grill.

"Look at the stomach on that guy," Tommy said. "Like *he* needs a steak."

The man left the Weber and went inside his house. Tommy stared through the fence. He said, "Wait here. I got an idea."

Tommy came back with a broom, a stickball bat, a kitchen fork and a roll of black electrical tape. He grinned and said, "Watch this. I'm a genius."

He taped the stickball bat to the broom, then taped

the fork to the bat. He said, "I'm going hunting. If you see that guy coming, say something fast."

Tommy got close to the fence, raised his steak harpoon and began lowering it toward the grill.

Nicky, peering through the fence slats, saw the back door open.

"He's coming!"

Tommy got the broomstick back just in time. The man in the Speedo came whistling across the yard, a beer in one hand, a plate and some tongs in the other. He set down the plate, poked the steaks a little and went back into the house.

Tommy draped his harpoon back over the fence and aimed. Stretching his arms all the way over, he jabbed at the steak—and got it. He lifted his harpoon and the steak rose off the grill just as the man in the Speedo came back into his yard.

"He's coming," Nicky whispered, grabbing the steak in both hands as it came over the fence. "It's hot!" Tommy shouted. "Run!"

When they were done eating, Tommy said, "That was the best steak I ever had. What a meal!"

"You think that guy will ever figure out what happened?"

"Not in a million years!" Tommy said. "We ate the evidence."

They went up to Tommy's room, and Tommy pulled a laptop computer from underneath his bed. "My prized possession," he said, and turned it on. The *BlackPlanet* logo appeared.

Nicky said, "How'd you get past the eighth level?"

"Easy," Tommy said. "You know when you're on the ice star? After you've destroyed the green ships, and there's the asteroid shower? You go Control X, Alt 5, and you get extra shields and rockets."

Nicky said, "That's not on any of the Internet cheats."

"No," Tommy said. "I think I invented it."

Tommy jumped to the eighth level and demonstrated. "See? Control X, Alt 5, bada boom, bada bingo. Here."

Nicky took the joystick and blasted away. The ninth level dawned like a sunrise. Nicky said, "Whoa."

"That's what I'm talking about," Tommy said. "Let's get out of here."

"Wait—is that the math homework?" Nicky pointed at a paper on Tommy's desk.

"Forget that," Tommy said.

Nicky looked at Tommy's clumsy writing. He said, "This geometry problem is easy. But you need the formula. Just like getting the cheats on *BlackPlanet*."

"Whatever. I don't get it."

" 'Cause you don't have the formula. Look," Nicky said, and pulled Tommy to the desk. "You're supposed to find the area of a circle, right? The formula is pi R squared. Pi is three-point-one-four. R is two. So, what's two squared?"

"It's four."

"Right. So what's four times three-point-one-four?"

"Twelve-something."

"Twelve-point-five-six," Nicky said. "So the area is twelve-something square inches. You work it out with a pencil and you're done! All the math stuff is easy, if you know the formula. You wanna do another one?"

"No—but thanks," Tommy said. "That's the first time I ever understood a math problem. So can we go now?"

When they were on the street, Nicky said, "Are we going back for more twenties?"

"More what?"

"Twenty-dollar bills. The guy in the candy store? We have to give him his change."

"Forget it. I took care of that already," Tommy said.

Night was falling, and the streetlights were coming on. Old people sat in the windows and on the stoops. Teenagers ran in the street. Cars cruised by, filled with boys looking for girls, and girls looking for boys. Tommy led Nicky down one block and across another until they were in an alley behind a large building with no windows. Tommy had to search for a while before he found what he was looking for: a metal doorframe. He pulled a screwdriver from his pocket and grinned.

"Here we go," he said, and began to pry the door open. It popped after a few seconds, and Tommy grinned again. "After you."

"Wait a sec," Nicky said. "Isn't this breaking and entering?"

"No," Tommy said, and pushed Nicky aside. "This is going to the movies for free. Step aside."

Tommy disappeared into the blackness on the other side of the door. Nicky waited. It *was* breaking and entering. Unless they didn't get caught. Nicky slid into the darkness. He said, "Tommy?" and when Tommy answered, he followed.

When they were inside, Nicky asked, "What movie is it?"

"How should I know?"

"You didn't check?"

"What for?" Tommy said. "It's free."

Two people were kissing, fifty feet high, right in front of them.

"Look at them," Tommy said. "It's disgusting."

"That's Harrison Ford," Nicky said. "I liked *Raiders of the Lost Ark*."

"This looks like *Raiders of the Old-Age Home*. It's stupid. Let's go."

When they were on the street, Nicky said, "How'd you know that door would be unlocked?"

"I know a guy who knows a guy."

On the way home, they passed the bakery where Grandma Tutti bought her cannoli. Tommy said, "Let's go see what old man Capaldi has," and pulled Nicky toward the back door.

"Is he open?"

"Capaldi is always open," Tommy said.

There were two men coming out the back door. One had a leather jacket slung over his arm. The other was carrying a toaster. He said, "Yo, Tommy."

"Hey, Mike," Tommy said, and they went inside.

The smell of damp yeast and baking bread was overpowering. Tommy led Nicky past two young men rolling out loaves of bread, into an office where Capaldi was doing figures on an adding machine. Capaldi looked up and grinned at Tommy.

"Heya, kid," he said. "What's shaking?"

"Not too much," Tommy said.

"Who's your friend?"

"This is Nicky," Tommy said. "He's okay."

"You from around here?"

"I'm staying with my grandmother and my uncle," Nicky said. "He's—"

Tommy jabbed him with his elbow, then said, "You still don't got no bikes, huh?"

"No," Capaldi said. "But I got some computer games. Let me see. . . ."

Capaldi glanced over his shoulder and around the

93

room. Nicky saw that boxes of TV sets, blenders and CD players were stacked against the walls. There was a rack of perfume. There was a rack of suits. There were boxes of Adidas and PUMA shoes.

"How about a wristwatch for your man Harvey?" Capaldi asked.

"Very funny," Tommy said. "You got any of that French brandy stuff?"

"Sure," Capaldi said, and went rummaging in a box. He came up with a bottle. "This ain't for you, right?"

"It's for my gramps," Tommy said.

"Five bucks."

Capaldi took Tommy's money and said, "I'll keep a lookout for that bike."

"Get two," Tommy said. "I could get Nicky to go for one."

In the alley, Nicky said, "What's with all that stuff? I thought he was a baker."

"He is a baker. And he sells stuff on the side."

"Is it stolen?"

"Not at all. It's just stuff that people bring him. Maybe a couple of toasters fell off the back of a truck. Or someone found some CD players sitting around at the docks."

"So it's stolen."

"No, no," Tommy said. "If it was stolen, someone

would be looking for it. This stuff, no one is looking for it. It gets lost, and Capaldi finds it."

When they were back in front of Nicky's grandmother's apartment, Tommy said, "Listen. With Capaldi, I stopped you from telling him who your uncle was."

"How come?"

" 'Cause of what your uncle does," Tommy said. "Not everybody thinks it's cool, what he does for a living."

"I understand," Nicky said.

"Not that I have a problem with it," Tommy said. "I admire the guy. But some people, they got an attitude, see?"

"Sure."

"Anyway, I'll see you."

Tommy waved the bottle of brandy and was gone.

CHAPTER NINE

There were four postcards the following day from Nicky's parents. They were written from four different islands, but were all postmarked from Barbados, and they all said the same thing.

We're having a wonderful time, the first one said. *St. Kitts is divine! Beautiful beaches and clear water. You'd love the kayaking.*

It's wonderful here, the second one said. *We're on St. Lucia. You've never seen such beaches! You'd love the papayas.*

From his father there was nothing. The idea of his dad trying to impress the boss—showing off with skeet shooting or bragging about winning some tough case—gave him a queasy feeling.

"What's the problem here?" Uncle Frankie said when he came down to breakfast. "Did something bad happen?"

"We had a call from Nicky's mother," Tutti said.

"Are they having fun on the cruise thing?" Uncle Frankie asked.

"They've decided to stay an extra week," Nicky said. "They want me to go up to camp, next week."

"You just got here!" Frankie said.

"You want to call and tell them that?" Tutti said.

Frankie thought for a second. "No. But why can't he stay here?"

"They think he should be up at camp," Tutti said.

"And what does *he* think? Is anybody asking Nicky?"

Frankie and Tutti turned to look at Nicky.

"I'd rather stay here," Nicky said.

"There you go," Frankie said. "Next time they call, you tell them, Ma."

Grandma Tutti rolled her eyes, crossed herself and said, "Sit down. Drink your coffee. I'll make some eggs."

Frankie left the house shortly after. Nicky walked out with him and said, "Are you going down to the social club?"

"Maybe not today," Frankie said. "I gotta see a guy about some stuff."

"Is it Mr. Capaldi?"

Frankie gave him a long look. "Even if you know about Capaldi, you don't know about Capaldi. You understand?"

Nicky nodded.

"I'm serious," Frankie said. "A lotta people think he's a good guy. In fact, *I* think he's a good guy. But we don't do business with him. Unless it's to buy bread. *Capeesh?*"

Nicky nodded.

"All right," Frankie said. "End of lecture. You got any plans for tonight?"

"No."

"We'll go out for a meal, you and me and your grandmother. Tell her I said to be ready about seven, okay? We'll do something nice."

Nicky had an ordinary day at school. Tommy was absent, again. The tedium was broken slightly in first period, when Frommer asked if anyone happened to know what the expression "pi R squared" meant. Nicky's hand went up before he thought about raising it. Frommer asked him to stand and answer. His face turned red, especially when he realized that Donna Carmenza was looking at him.

Donna came up to him during the morning break. "That was pretty sharp, with that square pie business."

98

"It's no big deal," Nicky said. "We studied it last year in math."

"It must be nice to be such a brain."

"I'm not a brain," Nicky said. "Not compared to some kids. And it's not all that nice, either. You get teased a lot. I'd rather be good at sports."

"That's stupid," Donna said. "Anybody can be good at sports. Being smart—that's special. So, are you going to be around for Santo Pietro?"

"What's that?" Nicky asked.

"It's the feast day of Saint Peter. And the church bazaar. It's like a big fair, but with *spedini* and *zeppoli* and sausage-and-pepper sandwiches."

"I'm not sure," Nicky said. "My parents want me to go back to camp. But I'd rather stay here."

"Then you should stay," Donna said, as if that settled it. "If you miss Santo Pietro, you'll miss me running the ringtoss booth. I bet you'd be good at that."

Nicky sailed through the rest of the day and then sailed home, thinking about playing games and winning prizes for Donna. He'd win her the biggest—

He heard the shouting before he even turned the corner. Mr. Moretti, the drunk who lived in his grandmother's basement apartment, was being attacked by two boys Nicky didn't recognize. Nicky broke into a run. His grandmother appeared on the stoop. He ran faster.

"Get out!" his grandmother was shouting. "Get out or I'll call the cops!"

She had the wooden spoon in her hand and was swinging wildly over the heads of the two boys. She landed a blow on one of them. He yelped, "Hey! Take it easy! He started this!"

The other boy was still pushing old man Moretti and slapping his face. Nicky charged at him and hit him in the chest with his shoulder. They both went down, hitting the sidewalk hard. Nicky felt the skin come off his knuckles.

The boy he'd tackled got to his feet and said, "Get away from me! Are you crazy?"

"Come on!" the other kid yelled.

They turned and ran.

Nicky and his grandmother got Mr. Moretti up off the pavement and led him down the steps into his dark, smelly apartment. Grandma Tutti pushed the old man onto a sofa that was missing most of its cushions and said, "Like I don't have enough trouble with you already, now you're brawling in the street in front of my building!"

"Mrs. Borelli, please! I'm an old man!"

"You're an old fool," Tutti said. "Next time you fight your own fight. Come, Nicky."

When they were upstairs, Grandma Tutti said, "It's going to hurt, but I'm getting the Mercurochrome." She came back with an old-looking bottle of medicine. "Hold your hand over the sink," she said, and then dripped orange liquid on his scraped knuckles.

Like fire! Nicky flinched. The sting brought tears to his eyes. His grandmother took his wrist and said, "Hold still, and don't be a baby." When she was finished, she said, "Come. I've got some of those nice cannoli left."

Frankie was home by five. He came up to Nicky's room, gave him a hug and said, "Hey, killer. Ma told me you gave a lesson to some hoodlums today."

"They were bullying Mr. Moretti," Nicky said. "I knocked one of them down, and they ran away."

"Good for you," Frankie said. "Although, the old man brought it on himself. He agreed to buy beer for those two kids. He bought wine for himself instead, and then refused to give the kids their money back. He's done it before."

Nicky put his face in his hands and said, "Oh, no."

"*Fugheddaboudit,*" Frankie said. "You did the right thing. You always gotta stick by your people, no matter what. I'm gonna see if I can find out who the kids were, and go talk to their parents. And return the money. They oughta know their kids are trying to get winos to buy them beer, for one thing. And Moretti oughta know he can't pull a stunt like that, at his age. But you—I'm proud of you. If someone is beating up

101

an old man, you gotta stop that, even if the old man isn't your downstairs neighbor."

Nicky was ashamed to say it, but he said it anyway: "I was scared."

"Of course you were scared! Two kids against one! That's scary."

"I guess that makes me sort of a coward," Nicky said.

"That makes you brave," Frankie said. "A guy who isn't scared, and starts fighting, what's brave about that? That's nothing. But a guy who's scared, and stands up for himself anyway? *That's* brave."

Nicky grinned and said, "Well, I wasn't completely alone. Grandma Tutti was going after them with her spoon."

"She's deadly with that thing!" Frankie said. "Listen, you get dressed, and we'll go out for dinner. You like Italian, right? Only kidding."

Dinner was a huge meal at a neighborhood place called Luigi's. Frankie had the *vitello*. His mother had the *pollo al limone*. Nicky ordered meat ravioli, in a meat sauce. It was heaven.

"Ma," Frankie said. "Look at him. Aren't you feeding the boy?"

"Night and day," his mother said. "But he's a teenager. You know what that is."

"I know what hungry is," Frankie said. "We better order dessert before he eats the tablecloth."

On the way home, Frankie said, "I remembered something, after the thing with old man Moretti. Me and your dad got jumped one night by these two clowns from another neighborhood. They were bigger than us, and since I was bigger than your dad, they went after me first. The fact is, I was getting beat. Then all of a sudden this one guy screams and jumps up, holding his leg. Then the other guy screams, and he jumps up, too. I look up and see your dad. He's got this piece of pipe, and he's smashing these guys on the backs of their knees."

"I never heard this story," Grandma Tutti said. "And I don't like hearing it now!"

"It was unbelievable," Frankie said. "I don't know why, but a sharp smack in the back of the knee is incredibly painful. The biggest he-man in the world will fall apart. How your father knew that, I don't know. But these guys started crying, and we took off."

"I can't believe my dad would do that," Nicky said. "He always told me you should never solve a problem with violence."

"That's a good rule—unless the problem *is* violence," Frankie said. "In that case, sometimes you gotta fight fire with fire. Or get beat up."

"What did the guys want from you?"

"Who knows?" Frankie said. "But we never saw them again. And your dad was the big hero for a couple of weeks."

The three of them walked the rest of the way in silence. When they got to the building, Frankie said, "I'll tell you something, Nicky. I miss your dad. I really do. Maybe now that you're visiting . . . Ah, maybe not. *Fugheddaboudit.*"

CHAPTER TEN

Tommy was back at school the following morning. At the break, he said, "Listen. This thing came up yesterday—a little job. A guy needs two kids to deliver some stuff. He'll pay us a hundred bucks."

"What for?"

"I didn't ask. He just said it was two packages. Take 'em in, drop 'em off, bang, we're done."

"That's a lot of money for nothing," Nicky said.

"I told him we'd meet him tonight," Tommy said. "I'll come to your place at seven."

In the afternoon Nicky went shopping with his grandmother. She was cooking baked ziti to take to a sick friend, plus a pot of *pasta e fagioli* for the house, plus a baked chicken *oreganata*.

"I need you to carry the chicken," she said. "There's something wrong with my arm."

"What's wrong with your arm, Grandma?"

"It's old, is what's wrong with it," she said. "I can't lift it up. Since yesterday morning."

"Does it hurt?"

"No. It just doesn't go up. It's tired."

"From what?"

"From talking! You, with the questions. Let's go to the store."

When they were back home, his grandmother said, "Here's what I want you to do. Wash the chicken, and pat it dry. Rub it all over with olive oil. Then sprinkle salt and oregano all over the outside of it, and mash two cloves of garlic and put those inside. *Capeesh?*"

"*Capito, nonna,*" Nicky said.

His grandmother smiled. "Now he speaks Italian! You're a good boy, Nicky. I'm going to lie down for a while."

Frankie came in an hour later. Nicky had finished with the chicken and was sitting at the kitchen table doing math homework.

"Hey, kid," Frankie said. "Where's Ma?"

"She's lying down."

"Lying down what?" Frankie said. "Ma doesn't lie down. I'm going to look in on her."

When he came back, Nicky said, "What did she say?"

"She said, 'I'm an old woman. What do you want from me?' She's gonna finish the ziti for Mrs. Giancola."

The chicken was unbelievable. Frankie ate four pieces. Nicky ate two. Grandma Tutti said, "Nicky used too much oregano. That's why it tastes so good. I should use more from now on."

"It's good," Frankie said. "Yours is good, too."

"This is better," she said.

The doorbell rang at seven. Nicky jumped up and said, "That's Tommy. I gotta go."

He gave his grandmother a kiss. His uncle grabbed him, got a hug and said, "Don't beat up any guys tonight, okay? The neighborhood needs a rest."

Nicky called out, "Bye!" and was down the stairs and out the door.

Tommy said, "Come on," and took off at a jog.

"Where are we going?"

"It's a few blocks," Tommy said, and kept running.

Around the corner they went, and over three streets, and up four blocks and over three more streets. They were in a neighborhood Nicky didn't know, and Tommy signaled to Nicky to stop running.

Tommy said, "You don't run down a block like this. Someone will think you stole something, and start running after you."

"What do you mean, 'a block like this'?" Nicky asked.

"Look. There's no one here."

It was true. The sidewalk was empty. There were no kids playing slapball, no kids on bikes or skates, no old men sitting on the stoops drinking wine.

Half a block down, they understood why. A grocery store with the windows busted out of it had bright yellow police tape stretched across the front door and the sidewalk.

"Something bad happened here," Tommy said. "Somebody musta got killed."

At the end of the next block, they turned left and stopped in front of a dry cleaner. It looked closed. But when Tommy pushed on the glass door, it swung open. The two boys went in.

The shop was dark and empty. A man stepped out from the shadows.

"Whatta you want?" he asked.

"We're here to see Jimmy," Tommy said.

"In the back," the man said, and pointed at a door.

Behind the door was an office. A man in a black suit with slicked-back hair was sitting with a phone stuck under his chin. He lifted his head at the boys' entrance and jerked his eyes toward a pair of seats against the wall. Tommy and Nicky sat.

The man said into the phone, "Tell him he's got two days. After that, we make meatballs out of him." Then he hung up. "Hiya, fellas. You're on time. I like that. You guys work together before?"

"We did a job for a guy passing bad twenties," Tommy said.

"No kidding," the man said. "And you're how old?"

"Uh, fourteen," Tommy said.

"You got a driver's license?"

"No."

"Too bad. I could use a kid with a driver's license," the man said. "If this job works out, maybe I can get you one. Here's the deal. I got two small packages I want delivered. But the guy who's getting them, he ain't around yet. They can't be delivered until Sunday. Some people have been snooping around here, asking questions. So I gotta move the stuff today, and get someone to deliver it Sunday. Got that?"

"Sure," Tommy said. "We hold on to it until then, and hand it over."

"Right," the guy said. "How much did I say it was?"

"You said a hundred—each," Tommy said.

The man in the suit grinned and his eyes lit up. He said, "No. I said a hundred, period. But I didn't know it was going to be two of you. Let's call it eighty—each.

Half now, and half next week, after the packages are delivered. How's that?"

Tommy said, "How about all of it, up front?"

The man's smile went away. "Don't hustle me, kid. Half now. Take it or leave it."

"We'll take it," Tommy said. "Where's the stuff?"

The man left the room and came back with two small packages wrapped in blue laundry paper and tied with string.

Tommy said, "That's it?"

"That's it, kid."

"It looks like dry cleaning. What's inside?"

"You don't wanna know. Just make the delivery, and come back for the rest of your dough."

"Where do we go?"

The man wrote down an address on a piece of paper and handed it to Tommy. "It's Jerry's Fish, on Twentieth Avenue. The guy's name is Dominick. He'll be expecting the package Sunday morning. Don't go near the place before Sunday. And don't hang around after you give him the stuff. Okay?"

"Okay," Tommy said.

"And don't screw this up," the man said. "Dominick is a very bad man. You don't want a guy like that mad at you. Or a guy like me, either. Don't forget that."

When they were on the street again, and off the block, Nicky said, "So whatta you think is in here?"

"The guy said we don't wanna know," Tommy said. "So I don't wanna know."

"But don't you want to guess?"

"No," Tommy said. "If it was nothing, he wouldn't be paying us to deliver it. So I don't wanna know."

Back at the apartment, Tommy said, "I've been thinking. Maybe you should hold on to these packages."

"Why me?" Nicky said.

"I don't know where to put them," Tommy said. "My mom comes in my room all the time."

Nicky said, "I guess I could put them in my room. I don't think my grandmother comes in there too much."

"Here," Tommy said, handing Nicky the packages.

Nicky tucked them under his shirt. "This stuff gives me the creeps."

"This stuff gives you eighty bucks," Tommy said. "Think of it that way."

Nicky let himself in and ran upstairs fast, calling out, "Hi, Grandma," as he went past the kitchen. He stuck the two packages in a drawer and buried them in T-shirts and underwear.

That night, trying to fall asleep, Nicky couldn't stop thinking about them. He imagined Grandma Tutti going through his drawers. He imagined her opening the packages. Worse, he imagined the police coming to the house. What was in there, anyway? What if it was drugs? He had nightmares about drug dealers and drug-sniffing dogs and policemen. He dreamed the packages got lost. He dreamed that—*Bang!* He woke with a start. It was time to go to school.

Decorations were already going up for Santo Pietro. Streamers and pendants were being hung across the street that separated the school from the church, where wooden booths were being constructed in rows that made the place look like a carnival midway. Port-O-Sans were parked in a line next to the street. Somebody was expecting a real crowd.

At the morning break, after math class, Donna found Nicky and took him across the street. Her booth sat below the church bell tower, facing the schoolyard. Nicky listened as Donna explained the complex inner workings of the ringtoss booth.

"Cool," Nicky said. "What can you win?"

"A bunch of crummy stuff," Donna said. "But one of the teddy bears is pretty good."

"That's what I'm going to win, then," Nicky said.

"I'd like to see that," a voice behind them said.

Nicky turned. It was Conrad—the kid who'd knocked him over on his first day of school, and who Tommy had said was Donna's old boyfriend.

"Hello, *Conrad*," Donna said.

"Hey," Conrad said. "You running the ringtoss again?"

"That's right."

"Remember last year? Who got the teddy bear then?"

Donna rolled her eyes. "You did, Conrad."

"And who'd I give it to?"

Donna rolled her eyes again. "Me."

"Maybe I'll do that again," Conrad said, and turned to Nicky. "Unless *you've* got other plans."

"I'm going to win it," Nicky said.

"Bet you won't."

"Bet I will."

"I'll see you here," Conrad said. "Weenie."

Nicky smiled and said, "Go for it. Take your best shot." Just like Rocky Balboa.

Tommy grabbed Nicky's arm as he was leaving the schoolyard after school.

"C'mere," he said, and pulled him around the corner. "Look."

It was *BlackPlanet Two*. The billboard had gone up in the night, huge over the top of the Berkeley Linoleum building at the end of the block. A vast black planet was rising, with twin moons orbiting it. Under the planet were the words "Coming in December: Dawn of a New Planet."

Nicky said, "*Awesome.*"

Tommy said, "*Unbelievable.*"

Nicky said, "But not until Christmas."

Tommy said, "Tell me about it. That stinks."

Nicky spent the afternoon in the kitchen with his grandmother, slicing garlic and stirring sauce for her famous steak *pizzaiola* with grilled peppers and onions. Between slicing and stirring, Nicky read the afternoon paper.

It was the usual junk: all kinds of bad things had happened all over. There was a photograph of the business with the blown-out windows and the police tape that he and Tommy had seen on their way to the dry cleaner.

"Police Suspect Arson, Murder in Fire," the headline said. The story explained that the cops were filing arson and murder charges in the disappearances of two men whose place of business had been burned down. Forensic investigators had determined that the two men, whose identities were not being released, had been robbed and perhaps kidnapped. Police said it was the third such fire and robbery of a small business in the past three months. They suspected that the killings were drug related, or the result of a turf war between rival Mafia gangs battling for control over territory.

The story was continued on page A-14. But there

was no page A-14. The pages went from A-12 to A-15 with nothing in between. Nicky could see that someone had torn the page out of the paper.

He was puzzling over that when the phone rang. Grandma Tutti was peeling the roasted peppers. She said, "Answer that, Nicky. It could be Frankie."

It was Nicky's mother. She sounded far away. "We're in Jamaica," she said. "It's beautiful here. But we're leaving. Guess why! Your father's been asked to become senior partner! That means he's got to get back to the firm *now*. We're flying home tonight. Since we're going home early, so are you. Clarence will be there for you Sunday morning. You can be at Camp Wannameka first thing Monday!"

"Does it have to be Sunday?" Nicky asked. "There's this big festival this weekend. The feast of Santo Pietro. I'd really like to stay for that. Can't I come home next week instead?"

He heard his mother put her hand over the phone. There was a long pause. Then she said, "Let me talk to your grandmother."

Tutti wiped her hands and took the phone. She said, "Hello?" and then listened. She scowled. She looked at Nicky and raised her eyebrows. Finally she said, "Of course he can stay. It's nice, Santo Pietro. His friends will be there. His new girlfriend, even. What difference does a week make, anyway?"

Tutti listened some more, then said, "Your father wants to talk to you."

Nicky took the phone. "Hello?"

"It's your father."

"Yeah. Hi, Dad."

"Your grandmother says you've been having a good time. Is that true?"

"Yes, sir."

"And she says you want to stay for the weekend, for Santo Pietro."

"Yes, sir. It's this big carnival thing, with rides and—"

"Please. I went to Santo Pietro every year. I was an altar boy. We had to build all the booths, and then we had to tear them all down. I *know* about Santo Pietro. Now, tell me about your uncle. Are you spending time with him?"

"We've been out to dinner," Nicky said. "Sometimes I go up to the Bath Avenue Social Club with him for a sandwich or something. He took me shopping for clothes. He—"

"He introduced you to the guys at the social club?"

"Sure," Nicky said, and then regretted it at once. Did his father know about Charlie Cement, and Sallie the Butcher?

"That's no place for a kid to hang around," his father said. "I don't want you going there anymore. And I

116

don't want you listening to Frankie too much. He means well, but the people he knows, and what he does for a living . . . you understand?"

"I understand."

"Okay. Now let me talk to your grandmother."

It was settled. Clarence would drive down Monday morning. Nicky could have the weekend, and Santo Pietro. When the negotiating was all done, Nicky went up to his room and lay on his bed. Monday was better than Sunday, but Monday seemed way too soon. And summer camp seemed so . . . lame. Noah and Chad and Jordan were nice guys and all, but he could hang out with them for fifteen years and not have as much fun as he'd had with Tommy in a couple of weeks.

On the other hand, there were the packages.

When dinner was almost ready, Grandma Tutti said, "Nicky, take the garbage down like a good boy."

Nicky carried the bucket downstairs and upended it into the trash can. A newspaper page was at the bottom. Nicky checked the page number: A-14. It was greasy and wet from being in the trash. Chunks of the paper tore away when he tried to unfold and read it. But he could see the words "Frank Borelli" and "police investigators" and "suspects kidnapped, dead or in hiding."

Kidnapped, dead or in hiding? It was incredible.

He and Tommy had stumbled onto the crime scene less than twenty-four hours, maybe, after his uncle had robbed the place. And killed or kidnapped the owners?

Nicky threw out the soiled newspaper and brought the trash bucket back upstairs.

Frankie was at the table when Nicky went back into the kitchen. He was wearing black jeans and a black sweatshirt and eating fast. He didn't look up when Nicky walked in. Then he put down his napkin and pushed his plate away.

"Good stuff, Ma, like always. I could eat four more plates. I'm sorry I gotta go."

"Where are you going?" Nicky asked.

"I got this thing," Frankie said.

"What kind of thing?" Nicky asked.

"A work thing," Frankie said. "Don't ask. I'll be back in a couple of days. Four-five days."

"Four or five days?" Nicky asked. "You're going to miss Santo Pietro."

"I know. I might."

"My folks came back early," Nicky said. "They're sending Clarence on Monday morning. You'll be back by then, right?"

Frankie frowned. "I don't know, kid. I might be. I'll

118

try. If I'm not, hey, you're from the neighborhood now. You can come and stay anytime you want. Maybe another week, later in the summer."

"Sure," Nicky said.

"C'mere," Frankie said. Nicky put his arms around his uncle's chest—and felt something. His uncle was wrapped in metal. He was wearing a bulletproof vest under his shirt.

Frankie said, "You're a good kid, Nicky Deuce. Let me get my stuff."

Frankie went down the hall and returned carrying his heavy gym bag. Nicky knew what was in that bag. He knew what his uncle was going off to do.

The kitchen was empty when Nicky got up the following morning. He poured himself a glass of milk and wondered where his grandmother had gone so early on a Saturday. When he had finished breakfast and she had still not appeared, Nicky went down the hall to her room.

Grandma Tutti was lying in bed, breathing heavily in the dark. Nicky put his hand on her shoulder and said, "Grandma? Grandma Tutti?"

She didn't wake up.

Nicky shook her shoulder gently and said her name again.

She didn't wake up.

Nicky shook her shoulder again, this time not so gently.

She didn't wake up.

Nicky ran out of the room, down the hall, into the kitchen. He had to get . . . *who?* Frankie was gone. He didn't know any doctor. He didn't know any neighbors. He tried to remember the names of his grandmother's old-lady friends. Gianfranco? Francomezzo? He couldn't think.

Nicky threw on his shoes and hurried downstairs and into the street, jumping over Mr. Moretti, who was sitting on the stoop, then ran around the corner to the Bath Avenue Social Club. He could ask Sallie the Butcher what to do. Or Oscar the Undertaker. No! Not him, of all people!

The door was locked, and the lights were out. Of course! Frankie was on a job. The guys would be with him.

Nicky ran back to the apartment. Rounding the corner, he nearly collided with Little Johnny Vegas, who grabbed him by the shoulders and said, "Hey, kid. Where's the fire?"

"It's my grandmother!" Nicky said. "I can't wake her up. I tried to get help, but—"

Little Johnny stuck his hand in the air. "Stop," he said. "I understand." He pulled out a tiny cell phone, pushed a button and said, "Yeah, it's me. We need a doctor, *fast*. Mrs. Borelli's house—852 Sixteenth Avenue. No ambulance or cops or nothing, right? Just a doctor. A'right."

Little Johnny stuck the phone back in his pocket and said, "C'mon, kid. Let's go meet the doc."

A black sedan was parked at the curb when they got there. A man in a black suit with a black medical bag got out. When he saw Little Johnny, he bowed and said, *"Buon giorno, Don Giovanni."*

"Hiya, Doc. It's this way. *Ascendere*. Up."

Nicky led them inside to his grandmother's room. The doctor sat on the edge of the bed and clicked on one of the bedside lamps. Nicky could see that his grandmother was still breathing. But when the doctor placed his hand on her forehead and then lifted her eyelid, she still did not wake. Nicky felt a sob rise in his throat. He left the room and went into the kitchen.

Little Johnny Vegas followed him. "Don't worry, kid. That doc is the best. He doesn't speak a word of English, but he's a real doctor. He'll take care of this."

"Okay," Nicky said. "Thank you, for helping."

"Forget it," Little Johnny said. "You got anything to eat?"

Nicky made the fat man a sandwich. The doctor came down the hallway a few minutes later, snapping his black bag shut, and took Little Johnny aside. They conferred quietly. The doctor glanced sideways at Nicky a few times and then went back into Tutti's bedroom. Nicky felt another sob rising in his throat. His grandmother was dying—he knew it.

Little Johnny Vegas sat down next to Nicky. "The doc says she's going to be okay," he said. "But she needs to get some tests. Something about her blood pressure—I think. My Italian is a little rusty on the medical stuff. We're going to use the doc's car to take her to Mary Mother of Mercy Hospital."

"I'm coming with you," Nicky said as Grandma Tutti emerged from her bedroom, leaning unsteadily on the Italian doctor's arm. He escorted her outside to his car.

Nicky grabbed his sketch pad and followed Tutti, Little Johnny Vegas and the doctor into the waiting car.

Nicky sat in the waiting room while his grandmother was examined, making sketches in his pad—the dark Italian doctor, Little Johnny Vegas, Tutti sleeping, the yellow man, the dry cleaner man, Tommy . . .

A hand on his shoulder woke him. A doctor with a name tag that read "Dr. A. Tannen" said, "Nicholas? Your grandmother is almost ready to go home."

"Is she going to be okay?" Nicky asked. "What's wrong with her?"

"Well, she has low blood pressure, and low blood sugar," the doctor said, "and she might have had a small stroke. But she's going to be fine, because you got her a doctor so quick. You saved her life, Nicholas."

Nicky nodded and felt tears coming into his eyes.

At the apartment they had to step around Mr. Moretti's sleeping, snoring body on the stoop. Grandma Tutti cursed under her breath—"*Ubriacone!*"—as they went inside.

"I'm going to lie down for a while," she said. "The doctor said I'm supposed to take three more pills at two o'clock. What time is it now?"

Nicky checked his watch. "It's one o'clock, almost."

"So come and get me in an hour, and we'll have some lunch," she said.

Nicky went through the kitchen, gathering lunch. There was a little prosciutto, and plenty of cheese. There was a melon. There was no bread. Should he run around the corner to the bakery? He was afraid to leave his grandmother. He wished Frankie was there. What if Tutti had died? How could he have found Frankie? His grandmother had a telephone-address book by the phone. Nicky went to it now and read the names listed under B. There were no Borellis except Nicky's family in Carrington. There was nothing for Frankie, or Frankie Borelli. Nicky closed the book.

Then he realized he had to tell his father what had happened. It was Saturday. His parents were supposed to have arrived home Friday. Nicky dialed his own house and waited.

The answering machine picked up and he heard his mother's cheerful voice. "You've reached the Borellis. Leave a message!"

After the beep, Nicky said, "Hi, Mom. Hi, Dad. Listen, uh, Grandma Tutti got sick. She was in the hospital for a few hours. It was a little scary. I was all alone here, and I didn't know who to call, and Uncle Frankie's not around, so . . . Well, anyway, she's okay. The doctor says she has to take it easy, and take some pills. I thought you guys would want to know. So that's it. Um, bye."

Nicky hung up. He opened his grandmother's telephone-address book again, to the first page. Inside the cover of the book was one telephone number, written in pencil, with no name beside it. Nicky thought, *I bet that's Uncle Frankie's cell phone number.*

He looked in on his grandmother. She was sleeping soundly. Nicky left the house, went around the corner to Capaldi's and bought a fresh loaf.

Tutti was up when he got back. She was drinking a coffee and arranging things on the kitchen table. She looked better.

124

"You made a nice lunch," she said. "And you're a nice boy, Nicky. I'm glad you were here this morning. With Frankie not being around, who knows what would have happened? Oh, and your father called. He got your message. I told him the whole story. He thinks you're a big hero. And so do I. Come here." Nicky gave his grandmother a big hug. "Now cut up a little bread and we'll eat."

That night, at his grandmother's urging, Nicky went out after dinner, walked to Tommy's house and knocked on the door.

"Whassup?" Tommy whispered when he opened the door.

"Nothing," Nicky said. "Can you come out?"

"Maybe," Tommy said, and glanced over his shoulder. "Give me fifteen minutes. Wait for me at the end of the block."

Fifteen minutes later, Tommy came strolling along, hands in his pockets, whistling.

Nicky said, "What was that about?"

"What was what?"

"How come you couldn't come out?"

"Grounded," Tommy said. "My mom got a notice from school. I might have to repeat math."

Nicky said, "It's none of my business, but you could ace that class if you just showed up. It's not like it's hard. I mean, I've seen you play *BlackPlanet*. That's way harder than anything we're doing in math."

Tommy said, "I don't know. I just don't get the problems."

" 'Cause you don't study," Nicky said. "It's easy, if you study. I'll help!"

Tommy nodded at him. "A'right," he said. "But not tonight. You wanna sneak in the movies?"

"Or we could even buy a ticket," Nicky said. "I've got some money. If we go in through the front door, we can see something we actually *want* to see."

"Okay," Tommy said. "Besides, we don't want anything to go wrong tonight, right before the big job tomorrow."

Nicky had forgotten. The next day was Sunday. It was Santo Pietro, and the delivery day for the two packages. The idea made him feel sick to his stomach.

"Come on," Tommy said. "I think there's something at the Criterion."

Nicky sat in the darkness and tried not to think about the packages. He tried not to think about Grandma Tutti alone in the apartment. He tried not to think about Uncle Frankie having to shoot his way out of some bank robbery.

It was a lot not to think about. Nicky tried to pay attention to the movie; it was a sci-fi story about some astronauts trying to repair their spaceship before their planet collided with an asteroid. Suddenly the movie was over and the lights were coming up and Tommy was laughing at him.

"You fell asleep!" he said. "You were snoring like an old man!"

"I guess I'm tired," Nicky said. "I'd better get home. My grandmother . . ."

"Come on." Tommy punched his shoulder lightly. "Let's get outta here."

CHAPTER ELEVEN

Sunday came. It was hot and muggy. Nicky lay in his bed, listening to the sounds from the street and worrying about the day to come. Then he smelled coffee and realized that his grandmother was up, too, and might need some help.

She didn't. She smiled and said, "There you are, sleepyhead. Are you going to make the marinara or not? I'm cooking the veal we didn't have yesterday."

"Sure," Nicky said, getting out the canned tomatoes. "I'm glad you feel well enough to cook."

"The day I don't feel well enough to cook," she

said, "you can start making the funeral arrange-
ments."

"Don't say that!"

"It's only the truth. How do you want your eggs—
scrambled?"

Donna had said to come to the ringtoss booth at noon.
Tommy had said to meet in front of the school at
eleven. Walking to early mass after breakfast, Nicky
told his grandmother that he'd be home for Sunday
supper at six.

"That's okay," she said. "You'll already eat a lot at
Santo Pietro. Sausage-and-pepper sandwiches. Rice
balls. *Zeppoli*. Cannoli . . ."

After church, back at the apartment, Nicky put
on his jeans and tennis shoes. He took the two packages out from under his clothes, then put them in his
backpack. On top of that he threw a sweater, his
math book, a *MAD Magazine* and his iPod, in case
anyone looked inside.

Then he stopped. He pulled one of the packages
out of his bag and put it on the bed. He thought, *What
if it's drugs, or guns, or something that will hurt somebody?*

He thought hard. *What would Tommy do? What
would Uncle Frankie do? What would a goomba do?*

Then he untied the string and opened the package.

It was a computer chip, small, the size of a half stick of gum. It had tiny writing on it. Nicky brought it up close to his eyes. It said *BP Two. Master.*

BlackPlanet Two! It was a bootlegged master copy of the new BlackPlanet game—the biggest computer game of all time. These chips were worth *millions*. Worth stealing. Worth killing for.

Nicky wrapped the package up, tied it with the string and shoved it down into his bag. He went downstairs and kissed his grandmother goodbye.

Tommy was waiting in front of the school. He caught Nicky's eye from across the street, and raised a finger to his lips—*"Shhh!"*

Nicky crossed the street. "What's going on?"

Tommy said, "Good morning." Then, under his breath, he said, *"There's a cop right behind you. Don't look!"*

Nicky didn't look. Tommy said, too loudly, "Come and see the ringtoss," and led him to the corner. Then Nicky turned. A uniformed policeman, walking his beat, headed for the church and Santo Pietro.

"He's leaving," Tommy said. "You got the stuff?"

Nicky nodded and said, "Listen, I opened one of them. It's not what you think it is."

"What do I think it is?"

130

"I don't know, but not this," Nicky said. "It's *Black-Planet Two*! Bootlegged master copies of the computer chip."

Tommy stared at the backpack. "That's serious. Let me see."

Nicky handed him one of the packages. Tommy quickly unwrapped it, whistled and wrapped it back up. "C'mon. Let's get this over with."

They left the school grounds, going away from the church. At the next corner, Nicky said hello to Mrs. Felco and two other women.

"Tell your grandmother Angela Cortona said hello," one said to Nicky.

A block on, Nicky was greeted by Mikey, who ran the corner store.

"Hey, yo, Nicky. Whassappening?"

"I'm running an errand for my grandmother."

"Good kid," Mikey said. "I'll see you around."

When they were away from him, Tommy said, "Do you know *everybody*?"

"It's not me," Nicky said. "It's my grandmother."

"And your uncle," Tommy said. "Turn left here."

Soon they were in a neighborhood that Nicky didn't know. There were fewer Italian names on the shops. The streets were emptier. There were no old men sitting on the stoops.

"Where are we?" Nicky asked.

"This is near where we met that guy with the fake twenties," Tommy answered. "That candy store is two blocks that way."

Nicky turned in the direction Tommy was pointing—and saw the man with the yellow skin standing next to an open car door, staring at the two boys.

"Tell me that ain't the guy," Tommy said.

"That *is* the guy," Nicky said.

"Hey!" the yellow man shouted. "Stop right there, you punks!"

Then he was running toward them.

Tommy took off down the block. Nicky ran after him. At the corner, Tommy said, "I'm going left. You go right. Meet me at the corner of Benson and Twenty-fifth. *Go!*"

Nicky, grateful that he'd put on his new black sneakers, tore down the next block. When he turned to look, he saw that the yellow man had turned left, too, and was catching up to Tommy.

Nicky couldn't run away. Suddenly afraid for his friend, he reversed direction and started running after Tommy and the yellow-skinned man.

After two blocks of running, Nicky had almost caught up to them. Tommy was nearing the corner. The yellow-skinned man was a half block behind him. Then Tommy fell. The blue dry cleaning package skidded away from him. Nicky saw Tommy grab the package. Then Nicky watched as the yellow man caught up and grabbed Tommy. Nicky turned and ran the other way.

He stopped at the next corner and hid behind a stoop. His heart was pounding and his chest hurt when he breathed. He was drenched in sweat. He wiped his face with his shirtsleeve and peeked around the corner. The yellow man was yanking Tommy down the block by his shirt collar. He had one hand stuck in Tommy's back, too—holding a knife, or a gun? What could the yellow man want? Could he know about the packages?

Then Nicky remembered. Tommy had told him they weren't going back to see the yellow man again. Nicky said, "We have to give him his change." Tommy answered, "I took care of that already."

Tommy had cheated the yellow-skinned man—and now this!

Nicky sat down and asked himself again, *What would a goomba do?* Well, he would not abandon his friend. He would not be afraid.

Nicky was no goomba. He was *very* afraid.

He started walking to Twentieth Avenue, to Jerry's Fish.

The front door was locked, and Nicky could see through the window that there was no one inside. He went to the end of the block, found an alley and followed that until he came to the rear of the fish store.

A man wearing rubber boots was washing out the inside of a panel truck with a hose. It smelled like dead fish. The man nodded at Nicky and jerked his hose at the back door.

It was dark inside, a big empty warehouse. Nicky could see light at one end. He went toward it, his shoes slipping on the wet concrete floor.

The light came from an office. Nicky pulled the door open and looked inside.

A middle-aged man in a cardigan sweater was sitting at a desk, talking on a cell phone. He waved Nicky inside and said into the phone, "Tomorrow morning. Five o'clock. I'll be waiting." He clicked the phone closed and held out his hand.

Nicky reached into his backpack, took out the blue paper package and set it on the desk.

The man looked at the package. "No good, kid. Where's the other one?"

Nicky took a deep breath. "We had a little problem. My friend, with the other package, he got attacked by this guy who maybe he owes money to. The guy took the other package. Now, I'm sure they're going to work it all out. And Tommy—that's my friend—I'm sure he's on his way here now."

"No good, kid," the man said. "Who's the guy that attacked him?"

"He's this guy with yellow skin and a long overcoat. He—"

The man held his hand up. "Kid, you're in trouble," he said. "Let me show you what happens to people who steal from people like me."

The man stood and grabbed the door of a big walk-in refrigerator. He pulled it open. A cloud of vapor escaped. Through the cloud, Nicky could see the body of a boy, frozen solid, standing in the cold. He gasped.

"Out," the man said.

The frozen boy took a step forward. He was holding a small package. It was Tommy.

"You too, you idiot," the man said. Nicky took his eyes off Tommy and looked back into the deep freezer. The yellow-skinned man, stiff and shivering, stepped into the little office. "You and that idiot dry cleaner, hiring kids to deliver this kind of merchandise! Little Johnny's going to cut your heart out."

The yellow-skinned man said, "D-d-d-dominick, you do-do-don't understand!"

"Shut up, you Popsicle," Dominick snarled. "And give me that package."

Tommy, shivering from the cold, dropped the blue package onto the floor. Then, bending down, he glanced at Nicky and winked. He tucked the package under his arm and squatted in a football stance.

Then he shouted, "Go, Nicky!" and shot to his feet and charged into Dominick. He hit the middle-aged man hard, waist high. The two of them crashed onto the floor.

Nicky ran out the office door and slid across the warehouse floor. He heard the door slam open behind him and turned to look. Dominick dashed into the warehouse after him. His leather shoes hit the slick floor, and he slipped and went down. Nicky dashed out the door and was in the alley.

He ran down the alley, onto the street and around the corner. He was halfway home before he realized no one was chasing him.

Why would they be? They had the packages. And a hostage.

There was a note from Nicky's grandmother on the kitchen table. She had decided to meet him at Santo Pietro.

Santo Pietro! Nicky had forgotten all about it. He had missed his ringtoss date with Donna. That creep Conrad had probably won the big teddy bear by now. His grandmother would be worried, too, when she didn't see him. But he had to go back for Tommy.

Nicky had an idea. He ran to his grandmother's telephone-address book. He opened it to the first page.

Grabbing the phone, he dialed the number penciled in on the inside of the cover.

The phone rang. Then there was a beep.

Nicky said, "Hello? Uncle Frankie?"

Nothing happened. He thought for a minute. He looked in the telephone book under *B* and found the number for the Bath Avenue Social Club. He dialed and waited. There was no answer. Of course. The guys would be out with Frankie, on the job. Nicky hung up and dialed the penciled-in number again. He got the same thing. It rang, then made another beep. Was it a pager number? Nicky hung up and hung his head.

There wasn't anybody else to call.

Except . . .

His dad had told him once, "If you're in trouble, you call me first. No matter what you've done, you always call me first."

Nicky went to his room and got his cell phone. He scrolled through his phone book until he found "Dad." It was his father's private cell phone line—for emergencies only. Well, this was an emergency.

His father answered on the second ring. "Borelli."

"Dad?"

"Nicholas! Is something wrong? Is it your grandmother?"

"No, Dad, Grandma's fine," Nicky said. "But I'm in trouble—serious trouble."

Nicky choked the words out—the packages, the yellow-skinned man, Jerry's Fish, the movie theater . . . everything.

"Okay," his dad said. "What's in the packages?"

"Computer chips, for a new game."

There was silence, then a sigh. "So, some local kid hired your friend Tommy to deliver these computer chips, and you got dragged into it."

"He's not a kid," Nicky said. "He's a gangster. He's holding Tommy hostage."

"Let's not exaggerate, Nicholas," his father said. "This guy isn't Don Corleone, and Tommy's going to be fine. Relax. I'll be there as fast as I can, and I'll get the whole thing sorted out. Okay?"

Nicky hung up. His eyes filled with tears. He remembered that it had taken Clarence almost forty-five minutes to drive him from Carrington to Brooklyn. This was going to be a long wait.

Nicky went back to the kitchen. He put the cell phone on the table, in case his father called back, opened his sketch pad and began drawing. He made a cartoon strip of himself delivering the package to Jerry's Fish, and the man in the cardigan, and Tommy and the yellow-skinned man in the deep freezer . . .

The knock at the door came sooner than he'd expected. Nicky dropped his pencil and ran to answer it. He yanked it open and yelled, "Dad!"

"Not quite." The yellow-skinned man reached inside and grabbed Nicky by the collar. "Come on."

There was a car waiting at the curb, with its back passenger door open. The yellow-skinned man hurled Nicky inside and slammed the door, then got behind the wheel and sped away.

In the dark warehouse, Tommy was sitting on the floor, in a corner, with his hands behind his back. The yellow-skinned man pushed Nicky into the corner and tied his hands behind his back, too. Then he walked off and disappeared into the warehouse office.

Nicky whispered, "Did they hurt you?"

"Not yet."

"What's going to happen?"

"I don't know," Tommy answered. "But it isn't going to be good."

"I called my dad. I told him everything. He told me to wait at my grandmother's house. But they came to get me before he got there."

"So now what?"

"I don't know," Nicky said. "He knows where we are. I told him Jerry's Fish, on Twentieth Avenue. I bet he's going to come here."

Tommy said, "Is that good? Is he, like, in the same line of work as Frankie?"

"He's a lawyer."

"A *lawyer?*" Tommy said. "We're dead."

Around four o'clock there was a knock at the warehouse door. Nicky stared into the darkness. The office door swung open again, and the yellow-skinned man walked across the warehouse floor. Blazing light poured in as he opened the door to the alley. Nicky could see the silhouette of a man. It was his father.

He whispered, "*That's him.* That's my dad."

Tommy said, "Great. I've almost got my ropes undone. How about you?"

"I haven't even tried."

"What have you been *doing* over there?"

"Nothing."

"Idiot. Grab my rope and tug on it. I think I'm almost untied."

Nicky shifted around. His fingers found one end of Tommy's rope. The end pulled free.

Tommy said, "Okay. Don't move. Let me try yours."

The yellow-skinned man led Nicky's father into the office, where Dominick was talking on the phone. Dominick nodded at a chair in the corner. Nicky's father didn't sit down. Dominick set the phone down and said, "Who the hell are you?"

Nicky's father said, "My name is Nicholas Borelli. I'm the father of one of the two boys you're holding in the other room. I'm here to take them home."

Dominick smiled. "Uh-huh. Just like that?"

"Just like that," Nicky's father said. "I don't think you understand the laws regarding kidnapping. I'm a lawyer, so I do. In this state, it gets you the death penalty. You're in an enormous amount of trouble. I'm here to get you out of it."

Dominick said, "You mean kidnapping is against the *law*? I had no idea. What's your offer?"

"I have people waiting for me to come out with my son," Nicholas Borelli said. "If I don't walk through that door in the next five minutes, they're coming in with cops."

"Let's see." Dominick lit a cigar and winked at the yellow-skinned man. "I let you go, in which case you run directly to the police, or I don't let you go, in which case the police come directly to me. Is that it? I think I'll save you the effort, and let the cops come *here*. Tie him up!"

The yellow-skinned man stepped forward, the rope taut in his hands.

Sitting on the floor, his own ropes almost free, Nicky heard the squeak of the warehouse door and saw a figure slip silently into the darkness. The figure moved across the warehouse floor and into the light coming from the office. Then Nicky saw. It was Clarence.

In the office, the yellow-skinned man said, "Turn around, pal." Nicky's father waited until the man's hand was on his wrists. Then he turned and hit the man hard across the windpipe. The yellow-skinned man fell to the floor, clutching his throat.

Just then Clarence burst into the office, leapt over the fallen body and crashed into Dominick. The two big men tumbled to the floor and the door slammed shut.

Nicky heard crashing furniture. Glass shattered. Someone grunted. Nicky's father called out, "Clarence!" and there was a gunshot. Then there was silence.

The office door swung open. Nicky's father came out first, his hands over his head. Clarence came out next. Behind them, holding pistols, came Dominick and the yellow-skinned man.

"Tie them up," Dominick said. "And try not to screw it up this time."

Dominick held the gun on Clarence and Nicky's father while the yellow-skinned man tied their hands behind their backs. When he was done, he shoved them roughly to the ground. Holding his throat, he kicked Nicky's father in the ribs and cursed quietly.

Then they were alone in the dark.

"Dad?"

"I'm okay," Nicky's father said. "What about you boys? Did they hurt you?"

"We're okay," Nicky said. "They tied us up. But we got our ropes off. We were coming in to help you guys."

"It's good you didn't," Clarence said. "They've got guns. They're willing to use them, too."

"So what do we do now?"

"We make a plan," Nicky's father said.

CHAPTER TWELVE

$\mathcal{F}$rankie Borelli was riding in the passenger seat of a panel truck that said "Hector's TV-VCR Repair" on the side. He said to the driver, "Pull over here, Danny. This is my mother's place."

"Sure thing, boss. I hope it's nothing serious."

"Two pages in five minutes? She's the only one who has that number. Believe me, it's serious."

Frankie jumped out of the car and sprinted across the street, house key in his hand. But the front door swung open. Frankie stuck the key into his pocket, pulled a pistol out of his shoulder holster and went inside.

The apartment was empty. Going into the kitchen, he called out, "Ma! You home?"

Nothing. He felt the stove, and the coffeemaker. Cold. He checked his mother's bedroom. Empty. He checked Nicky's bedroom. Nothing.

Back in the kitchen, he noticed three things. First, his mother's telephone-address book lay open on the counter. Frankie picked up the phone and pushed the redial button. The pager clipped to his belt began to beep. He said, "Okay. That explains that."

Second, there was a note from his mother to his nephew and a cell phone lying on the kitchen table. He punched the redial button. The other end rang, and a voice said, "This is Nicholas Borelli. Please leave me a detailed message."

Frankie put the phone in his pocket and said, "Okay. Ma's fine, but Nicky's involved."

Third, he noticed Nicky's sketch pad open on the kitchen table. He saw Nicky's drawings—the yellow-skinned man, the dry cleaner, the man in the cardigan sweater, the boy delivering the package. He saw Nicky's drawings of Tommy, and Little Johnny Vegas.

He said, "That's what's going on."

He took a notepad off the counter and wrote a note. *Ma: Nicky's in a jam. I'm going after him. Don't call anybody—especially me, on my pager. If I'm not back tomorrow morning, call Jeff Tomlinson. Tell him to come see you. Show him Nicky's sketch pad. I love you. Frankie*

Frankie locked the door behind him and went down the stairs. Nutty was standing at the bottom, dressed like a naval cadet, in white shirt and pants and a peaked cap. He snapped to attention. Frankie stopped and saluted. He said, "Ensign Nutty. Do you have anything to report?"

"Sir, yes sir! Your nephew, leaving the house under protest, *sir!*"

"Was he with a guy with stringy hair and yellow skin?"

"Sir, yes sir!"

"Did they walk away, or drive?"

"They drove, sir!"

"Can you describe the car?"

"Black Montego, sir! New York license A-six-six-eight-two-oh-seven, sir!"

"Excellent work, Ensign Nutty. At ease!"

Frankie jumped back into the panel truck and dialed a number on his cell phone. "What can you give me on New York plate A-six-six-eight-two-oh-seven?"

He waited.

"Yeah. I know him. Thanks."

He put the phone away and said, "We gotta make a call on Dominick Pavese."

"Little Johnny's guy?"

"Yeah. It ain't no social visit, either. I think we'd better dress up."

Frankie moved to the back of the panel truck. He rummaged around and came up with two Kevlar bulletproof vests. He handed one to his partner and said, "Put this on. I'm going to try to get my brother on the line."

Danny said, "You have a brother?"

"I used to," Frankie said.

Nicky's dad shifted on the floor and looked at Tommy. "Is this the guy who got you into this?"

"Not really," Nicky said. "I kind of got myself into it."

His father looked at them, then around the warehouse, and said, "Well, we're all in it now. These guys are very serious. Tell me what you know about them. Quietly."

When they were done, Nicky's father said, "Okay. It sounds like they're waiting for something to happen. Do you know what it is?"

"There's a delivery coming in the morning," Tommy said. "I heard them talking about it before they caught Nicky. . . ."

A cell phone rang. Nicky's father said, "Damn! That's my phone. I can't get it with my hands tied."

"I can," Nicky said. He slipped his hand into his father's jacket pocket, pulled the phone out and flipped it open. The ringing stopped. Several minutes later it started again.

The yellow-skinned man came out the office door, shining a flashlight across the floor in front of him. Nicky dropped the phone and stuck his hands behind his back.

"What was that sound?" the yellow-skinned man asked.

"It was from outside," Nicky's father said. "There must be a church near here."

"There's no church near here," the man rasped. "It's all warehouses."

"There's gotta be a church near here. There's a church near everywhere," Nicky's father answered.

The yellow-skinned man moved forward and pointed the flashlight at Nicky's father's face. "There isn't no church around here, damn it!"

"I bet you're wrong," Nicky's father said—loudly. "We're by the corner of Twentieth Avenue and Bayview, behind Jerry's Fish, right? In Bensonhurst? I bet there's a church at both ends of this block. And I don't care if you guys *do* have guns."

"Shut up, you!" the yellow-skinned man said, and smacked Nicky's father across the face with the flashlight. Nicky's father fell over sideways.

Nicky screamed, "Leave him alone, you coward! Pick on someone—"

"Keep talking, you midget," the yellow-skinned man whispered. "In a couple of hours you'll be talking to the angels."

He went back across the warehouse and pulled the office door closed behind him.

Nicky put the phone in his pocket and took his father's face in his hands. "Dad! Are you all right?"

His lip was bleeding, but he smiled. "I'm all right, especially if the person calling on that cell phone heard the stuff about the churches."

Clarence said, "Mr. Borelli! You were doing all that on purpose!"

"What do you think, I was just taunting the guy so he'd hit me?" Nicky's father grinned.

Three minutes later, the phone rang again. This time the yellow-skinned man came out at once.

"Now I get it," he said. "Church bells! Very cute. Who's got it?"

He found the phone in Nicky's pocket.

"Very cute," he said again, and stuck the phone in his pocket. "Church bells! Don't make me come back out here."

In the panel truck, Frankie put Nicky's cell phone back in his pocket. He said, "My brother is a genius, and I know where he is. It's Jerry's Fish—Dominick Pavese's place—on Twentieth. But he's not alone, and the people he's with are not going to like being interrupted. Let's move in slow."

It was a long night. The concrete warehouse floor was cold and uncomfortable. Tommy and Clarence fell asleep. Nicky and his father sat with their backs to each other—his father watching the office door while Nicky worked at untying his father's ropes.

"That was some trick with the phone," Nicky said.

"Lucky shot," his father said. "It would help if I knew who was calling."

"Could it have been Mom?"

"Not likely," his father said. "But it might've been my assistant. He's very sharp. Worked in the district attorney's office. *He'd* figure out where we are."

"I tried calling Uncle Frankie, on his cell phone, but I couldn't reach him."

"He probably can't carry a cell phone, in his line of work."

"So, you know all about that, huh?"

"About Frankie?" His father turned and looked at him. "Of course I know. And I hate it. It's unfair to my mother, to put her through that kind of stress. It's terrible."

Nicky thought of his grandma Tutti, at home, alone, not feeling well, one son on the run from the police after a botched robbery, the other son and her grandson being held captive and almost certain to be killed at dawn.

Holding back his tears, Nicky said, "I think I almost have your rope undone."

"Good boy," his father said. "Maybe I can get Clarence freed up."

"And then what?"

"No idea," his father said. "First let's get the rope off."

It was another hour before Nicky got the rope untied. His father pulled his hands free and sat rubbing his wrists. He shook Clarence awake and said, "Turn around. I'm going to get the knots undone, and we're going to get out of here."

Tommy woke up, too. He said, "I had a dream. I think I have a plan."

Nicky and his father turned to him. Nicky's father said, "Is that so?"

"It's from *BlackPlanet*," Tommy said. "Nicky, you know in level six, there's that alien city where you have to use the photon blasters to knock out the force shields?"

"Yeah?"

"I found a mistake in that level. If you unload everything on the first force shield, the other three collapse and you can zip right out. Same thing here, right?"

Nicky's father said, "I think we need a *real* plan."

"This *is* a real plan," Tommy said. "They got one

door going in and out. They can't watch us and watch the door at the same time, right? So if we unload everything we got on the door—boom! One of us will get out and get the cops."

"Unload everything we got?" Nicky's father said. "We don't 'got' anything."

"I bet there's all kinds of stuff in here," Nicky said. "All we need to do is make a diversion, right? We can find something to do that with. Let's look around."

"Okay," his father said. "But quietly."

Nicky went off into the dark warehouse on his hands and knees. He came across something that felt like an old tennis shoe. In a far corner, he found a water spigot, and a plastic bucket. He found a piece of metal that felt like part of a tire jack. He took that back to the others.

"There's a faucet and a bucket in that corner," he told his father. "Plus I found this metal thing."

Nicky's dad hefted the metal bar. "It's a lug wrench. That could come in handy."

A few seconds later Tommy came crawling from the opposite direction. He said, "I found a piece of pipe, and a stickball bat."

He handed them over. Nicky's father picked up the pipe. Then he said, "Nicky, fill that bucket up with water and bring it back. Carefully. Don't spill any of it on the floor. Okay?"

"Okay."

"Tommy? You're going to take the lug wrench over to that big sliding door and see if you can pry it open. Check it out and come back. Okay?"

Tommy said, "Okay. But what if—"

"Shhh," Nicky's father said. "Don't talk. Nicky, go."

Nicky went across the pitch-black warehouse, creeping along until he found the water spigot. The faucet opened like Niagara Falls, the sound roaring through the empty warehouse. Nicky turned it off at once and held his breath. Then there was silence. He started again, slowly. When the bucket was full, he crept back across the floor.

Tommy came back just then, too. He said, "I can get the door open, but it's going to be loud."

"That's okay," Nicky's father said. "By the time we're moving, it won't matter."

Frankie and his partner stood behind Jerry's Fish. Frankie noted the heavy sliding doors, the transom windows above, the low roof.

He said to Danny, "Any ideas?"

"Smash in through the windows?"

"I don't like it," Frankie said. "There's at least two guys in there, and they've got guns, and hostages."

"So what's the alternative?"

"Let's see if we can get in from the roof." A ladder at the end of the building led them to the rooftop.

Searching in the dim light, they found a skylight, held down by a padlock.

"You got a bolt cutter?"

"Yeah," Danny said.

Frankie broke the lock and tested the skylight. It opened freely.

They both drew their weapons. Frankie peered in through the skylight, pistol poised to fire.

"It's clear," he said. "Put on your ears."

Frankie and Danny reached into their bags and pulled out headsets. Frankie clicked his on and said, "Can you hear me now?"

"Very funny," Danny said, adjusting his own headset. "I hear you fine."

"Good. Then let's go. Radio silence for the first few minutes. Call me when you get ready."

Danny looped a rope around his chest and knotted it, then gave the other end to Frankie, who held the rope tight as Danny dropped himself through the skylight. Frankie felt the line go loose when Danny hit the floor.

When they were ready, Nicky's father said, "Here's the plan. We're going over by the office door. Tommy's going to be on the sliding door with the lug wrench. I've got the pipe. Clarence has the stickball bat. Nicky, you're going to yank open that office door and yell something, then close the door and wait. Tommy's going to lever the sliding door open. Nicky, you're going to pour that bucket of water on the floor. When it's wet, it's going to be as slick as ice. The two guys will come tearing out here. They'll hit the wet floor and *wham!* They go down, and Clarence and I smack 'em."

"It's an awesome plan," Tommy said.

"It's a *Three Stooges* plan," Nicky's father said. "But it could work. The whole thing depends on timing. And silence. Let's go."

Nicky's father showed them their positions. Tommy went down to the door and wedged the end of the lug wrench into it. Clarence stood facing the office door with the stickball bat. Nicky's father stood with the piece of pipe. Nicky held the bucket of water. Nicky's father held his hand up: *Wait.*

They waited.

Ten minutes later, Frankie was in the alley, staring up at a pair of transom windows. He clicked on his headset and said, "Talk to me, Danny."

The headset crackled. Then: "I'm here. I see an office with two guys in it."

"And the others?"

"I can't see them."

"Keep looking," Frankie said. "They could be inside the refrigerators. They could be meat by now." Frankie

155

shuddered. "Forget I said that. I'm going to try the door. Maybe we can get them in a crossfire."

"Got it."

Frankie walked to the sliding door. He pushed, and it made a creaking noise. He tested again. More noise. He said, "So much for the surprise attack."

Then he heard something. Was it coming from inside? He put his ear to the door. Nothing. He turned and looked down the alley.

There it was—a low rumbling, coming from somewhere in the neighborhood. It sounded like a truck engine. Frankie stared at the end of the alley. Headlights. Getting brighter. Turning toward the alley.

Frankie dropped his gym bag onto the pavement and said into the headset, "Yo, Danny! We got company! I'm going with the grenade now—on three. Copy?"

Danny's voice crackled. "Copy."

Frankie pulled a percussion grenade out of his gym bag and placed his hand on the sliding door. He said into the radio, "One-two-THREE!"

On "three," Frankie shoved the sliding door open, jumped inside and threw the percussion grenade toward the lighted office. He dove onto the floor as the grenade went *BOOM!* and exploded daylight across the darkened warehouse.

Nicky jerked as if he'd been electrocuted, and covered his eyes. His father said, "Get down!" Nicky dropped his bucket and spilled two gallons of water onto the floor.

He heard the office door swing open. The yellow-skinned man said, "Hey!" and Nicky heard him slip and hit the floor. There was the crunch of a pipe, then the crack of a bat. The door flew open again. Nicky saw the silhouette of Dominick slip and fall hard. Then he heard his father's grunt, and another crack of the bat.

The warehouse lights came on. A voice screamed, "Freeze! Nobody moves!"

Nicky's father, lying on the floor and clutching his leg, said, *"Frankie?"*

"Get down, Nicky! Stay down!" Then Frankie shouted into his headset, "Danny! Get me some backup!"

In the alley, two car doors slammed.

Dominick got to his feet and shouted, "Jimmy! Mackie! We got trouble!" He kicked Clarence, who was lying on the floor, and turned toward the empty warehouse.

Nicky saw his shot. He grabbed the stickball bat from the floor, swung hard and connected with the back of Dominick's right leg. The big man crumpled, moaning.

A second later, a man holding two automatic pistols stepped out of the shadows. He said, "Nice shot, kid," quietly, then shouted, "Yo, Frankie! On your back! Everybody down *now!*"

The man with the pistols began firing past Frankie, at the sliding door. Nicky hit the floor. He saw Frankie drop to his knees and spin and begin firing. Nicky pressed his face into the concrete. Bullets flew over his head and ricocheted off the block concrete walls behind him. Then he heard something else—a *thunk-thunk*—and turned to see the man with the two pistols fall over. There was more gunfire. The roar was deafening.

Then it was silent.

Frankie shouted, "I'm going after 'em, Danny. Get the backup!"

Danny didn't answer. Frankie didn't wait. He ran for the sliding door screaming into his headset, "Code Four! Code Four! Man down!"

The yellow-skinned man jumped to his feet and began running for the door, too. Tommy leapt up and dashed after him. Just as the man got to the sliding door, Tommy dove and tackled him from behind. Nicky heard the man's head smack the floor like a ripe melon.

Frankie dashed into the alley. The piercing wail of police sirens sliced through the night. Headlights lit both ends of the alley, silhouetting the forms of two men running toward Bayview.

Frankie shouted, "Freeze! Police! Freeze!"

The two men came to a sudden halt and raised their

hands over their heads as a dozen police officers stepped from behind the police car headlights, their weapons poised and ready.

Inside, Nicky looked across the warehouse. His father held the pipe over the moaning Dominick. Clarence, with blood on his forehead, was sitting on top of the yellow-skinned man. Nicky said, "Is that the police?"

"Yeah," his dad said, and smiled. "And just in time, too."

"But, what about Frankie?"

His dad said, "He's okay."

"Isn't he going to get into trouble?"

"Maybe so. He should've called for backup earlier."

Nicky was confused. He said, "Who should've called for backup?"

"Frankie should've. Or his partner. Even for an undercover detective, that's standard police procedure."

Nicky was even more confused. "Detective? Uncle Frankie is the *police?*"

"Of course he's the police!" his father said. "What'd you think he was?"

"I thought he was a gangster."

Hours later, Nicky and his grandmother and his father and his uncle sat in Grandma Tutti's kitchen. The two men had coffee mugs. Nicky had a glass of milk. The table was strewn with the remnants of a big breakfast.

Nicky had told everyone everything and had apologized for causing so much trouble. Nicky's grandmother had told her two sons all about her visit to the hospital and how Nicky was her hero. Nicky's father had told his brother about showing up at Jerry's Fish and getting hit in the leg while trying to overpower Dominick Pavese.

Frankie started laughing. "Now I see the family resemblance, with the two of you," he said. "Big Nicky goes *boom* on the one guy's leg, and Nicky Deuce goes *boom* on the other guy's leg. Like father, like son. You took 'em *both* out."

"With Clarence and Tommy for backup," Nicky's father said. "Some team!"

"Where did Clarence go, anyway?" Frankie asked.

"I sent him over to the hospital with your partner, to get that cut on his forehead examined."

Nicky said, "Is Danny going to be okay?"

"The Kevlar stopped four rounds," Frankie said. "The fifth one grazed his shoulder. It's a parking ticket. They'll send him home tonight."

"He's lucky. We're all lucky!" Nicky's father said. "When that flash grenade went off, I thought we were all dead guys."

Nicky said, "Me too. I was scared. When I heard the

160

siren, I thought the police were coming for *you*. I thought maybe you were part of Dominick's gang."

"What's that all about?" Frankie said. "What's with this idea that I was some kind of mob boss?"

"I don't know," Nicky said. "You talk like the people in *The Godfather*, and *The Sopranos*. Plus there's all your friends, with the gangster names—Sallie the Butcher, and Oscar the Undertaker, and Jimmy the Iceman. And Bobby Car Service."

Frankie laughed. "What an imagination! Sallie *is* a butcher. Oscar runs a mortuary. Jimmy owns an air-conditioning company. Bobby runs a livery car service. What'd you think they did?"

"I thought Oscar killed them and Jimmy froze them and Sallie cut them up and Bobby drove the getaway car," Nicky said. Then he remembered something else. "If you're not gangsters, what about that time I came to the social club and you guys were all making notes and planning on getting the blueprints of some bank vault, and talking about casing the joint?"

Frankie thought about that and stared at his brother and Nicky, then said, "That was no bank vault. That was Scarantino's wedding hall. We were planning Sallie's wedding!"

"I thought it was a bank job," Nicky said.

"The imagination on you!" Frankie said. "We're planning a wedding, and he thinks it's a heist."

"What about the job in Arizona?" Nicky asked. "And what about that shoot-out over on Twenty-sixth Avenue? Was that a wedding, too?"

Frankie got serious. "No," he said. "Those were for real. The guy in Arizona had a tip for me about electronics being hijacked from airports on the West Coast and moved into cities on the East Coast. We set up a sting operation, and it went bad. A couple of guys got shot."

"I read about that in the newspaper," Nicky said. "I saw your name."

"How?" Tutti asked. "I tore that page out and put it in the trash."

"I found it, when I took the trash downstairs," Nicky said. "But it didn't say Uncle Frankie was a policeman."

"And it didn't say who the ringleader was, either, did it?" Frankie asked.

"No," Nicky said. "But, was it Dominick?"

"The kid's a genius!" Frankie said. "Speaking of which, that's some sketchbook you got there." He turned to his brother and said, "I hope you realize what a talent this kid has. Without that sketchbook, I never woulda figured any of this out. It was like a road map."

"He's a real artist," Grandma Tutti said. "You should see the drawing he did of me in the kitchen. Like a regular Rembrandt."

"I saw that one," Frankie said. "And I got a look at the little cookie, too."

Nicky said, "What cookie? What do you mean?"

"The cream puff," Frankie said. "*The girl*. In the sketchbook."

"That's Donna Carmenza," Grandma Tutti said. "Nicky's girlfriend. She was asking where you were, at Santo Pietro. I told her to stop by the house after she was done."

"You asked her to stop by *here?*" Nicky asked.

"She said she would come by after lunch."

"You should get that Tommy over here, too," Nicky's father said. "Him with his plan for busting out of that warehouse. He's a smart kid, that one—a troublemaker, but smart."

Nicky clapped his hand over his mouth and gasped.

His uncle said, "What?"

"Tommy . . . I just thought of something," Nicky said. "After the police came in, and put the handcuffs on those guys . . ."

His uncle said, "Yeah, what?"

"What happened to the packages?"

Nicky's father said, "Tommy's got the computer chips!"

"He tricked us!" Frankie said, and started laughing.

"Those chips are worth millions," Nicky's father said. "Does he have any idea how valuable they are?"

Frankie and Nicky stared at him.

"Okay, stupid question," he said. "Of course he knows. What're we gonna do?"

Frankie laughed. "Keep your shirt on. I'll go see the little thief later today, and give him a smack."

"I'm gonna see about getting him a job," Nicky's father said. "First he's an entrepreneur, with all these little scams. Then when he gets caught, he comes up with the diversion plan. Then he tackles the crook while he's running for the door. And when no one is paying attention, he makes off with a million dollars' worth of computer chips! A guy with that kind of brains shouldn't be running loose in the streets."

"He should be a lawyer," Frankie said.

"Or an undercover policeman," Nicky's father said.

"Someone shoulda been watching him," Frankie said.

"Someone shoulda been watching *both* these boys," Nicky's father said.

"I'm sorry," Nicky said, and hung his head. "I guess I didn't turn out to be such a goomba after all."

"What are you talking about?" his uncle said. "You did great! Your grandmother got sick, and you saved the day. Your friend got caught, and you went back for him. You got into a jam, and you fought your way out. You were a great goomba!"

"Which is not always the best thing to be," Nicky's father added. "I'm glad you connected with your uncle and your grandmother and your culture and all that, but you also acted like a hoodlum. We'll have to have a long talk on the drive home about how you spent your summer vacation."

"Take it easy, Nicky," Frankie said. "So he got into a little trouble. It happens to kids all the time."

"Not like this," Nicky's father said. "He was passing bad twenties. He was busting into movie theaters. He was attempting to deliver a package of stolen merchandise, for a known criminal. He and his friend—"

"Easy," Frankie said. "That kind of thing can happen to anybody. Like, to you, for example."

"To me?" Nicky's father looked surprised. "Not like that. Never."

Frankie smiled. "You sure? Have you forgotten Stinky?"

Nicky's father said, "Stinky Savonara? What about him?"

"You remember him, that summer, with the softball equipment?"

"No," Nicky's father said, and glanced at his mother.

"You liar! You do!" Frankie said, then turned to Nicky. "Stinky Savonara's father was a longshoreman. He worked down at the docks. And every once in a while a shipment would come in that interested Stinky—and some of it would, you know, disappear. One summer Stinky and your dad and me and some other guys were all playing softball. We wanted to be a summer softball league team. But we didn't have any uniforms. You couldn't be a league team with no uniforms. So what does Stinky's father find in a shipment? Uniforms! Red and white! Beautiful! With a team name already sewn onto them. So, Nicky here gets the idea to pinch the uniforms and the team name. Overnight, we became the Rimfield Rockets! Hurray for the Rimfield Rockets!"

Nicky's father put his face in his hands and said, "I had forgotten this."

"I'm not done," Frankie said. "The plan worked. We got into the league. So what happens at our very first league game? We meet the *real* Rimfield Rockets, a team from Rimfield, New Jersey—and their sponsor was the Rimfield Police Department! They came after us like gangbusters, with their fists and their bats. We ran off the field so fast we left behind our mitts and gloves and bats and everything!"

Grandma Tutti said, "I never knew why you boys quit softball that summer."

"So much for Mr. Goody-Two-Shoes Nicky," Frankie said. "So give your son a break, huh? He's a hero! He caught the bad guys."

"Okay," Nicky's father said. "Here's to the hero, then."

He lifted his coffee mug and said to Nicky, "*Salute.*" Then he turned to his brother and said, "And, thanks."

"Hey, thank *you*," Frankie said. "There was trouble. Nicky called. And you came! You're a hero, too. This is turning out to be some reunion."

Nicky smiled. "Yeah, welcome to the family, Dad."

Grandma Tutti turned from her stove, wooden spoon in hand. "It's not like I imagined it—but it's good," she announced. "My sons are together again, arguing like brothers. Little Nicky is here with his father. It's like the old days: me and all my boys, in my kitchen, around my table, in my house."

"Ma! Stop crying!" Frankie said. "You're gonna wreck the marinara."

"Finish your breakfast," Grandma Tutti said. "And, Nicky, you should get cleaned up, in case Donna Carmenza comes over. Besides, I gotta start cooking lunch."

Grandma Tutti's Tomato Sauce
(aka "Gravy," or Sunday Sauce)

This is the basic recipe for the most basic sauce in Italian cooking. This is the marinara. This is the root. All other recipes grow out from this one. If you can do this, if you can do only this, you can qualify for goomba status in the kitchen. If you can't do this, you are not going to make it. Order out, or whatever.

This is the sauce that goes on all noodles—macaroni, spaghetti, linguine, whatever. You can call it pasta sauce if you want. But don't, if you want to be a goomba. No goomba calls it "pasta." That's a word they use in Italy. In America, it's a yuppie thing. Not for serious people. You say "macaroni" or "spaghetti." The end.

This is also the sauce that you use to build your lasagna, your manicotti, your sauce with meatballs, and a hundred other goomba meals. Get this right, and you got the whole thing.

For starters, just try making the sauce and putting it over noodles. Nothing fancy. No osso bucco yet. No baked rigatoni. Just macaroni. It should taste pretty good, just like that, with a little hard-crusted Italian bread, and a little Parmesan cheese grated over the top. If it doesn't, again, clear out. You got no business cooking this stuff—or even eating this stuff.

SERVES 4

3 tablespoons olive oil
1 garlic clove, minced
1 28-ounce can tomatoes with their juices, diced
2 tablespoons chopped fresh basil or ½ teaspoon dried

¼ teaspoon sugar
¼ teaspoon salt
1 tablespoon olive oil
1 pound spaghetti

Heat 2 tablespoons of the oil in a saucepan over medium heat until it becomes fragrant. Mix the garlic with one teaspoon of water and carefully add this to the warm oil. Sauté the garlic and cook without browning it. Add the tomatoes, bring to a boil, then reduce the heat. Simmer for 10 minutes. Add the basil, sugar and salt, and simmer 5 more minutes. Just before serving, blend in the last tablespoon of olive oil.

SPAGHETTI WITH SAUCE

Heat four quarts of water in a big pot. When it is boiling, add the spaghetti. Cook the noodles 11 to 13 minutes, depending on how al dente you want them to be. When they are right, drain the noodles in a colander. Drain them completely.

Serve the spaghetti in a big bowl, with the tomato sauce poured on top. Serve with bread and grated Italian Parmesan cheese. *Salute!*

STEVEN R. SCHIRRIPA is best known to television audiences as Bobby "Bacala" Baccalieri on the HBO hit series *The Sopranos*. He has also become a regular field correspondent for *The Tonight Show with Jay Leno* and appeared as host for Spike TV's *Casino Cinema* series. Steve is developing a half-hour situation comedy based on his bestselling book *A Goomba's Guide to Life*, coauthored, along with *The Goomba's Book of Love* and *The Goomba Diet*, with Charles Fleming. Steve lives with his wife and their two daughters in New York City and Las Vegas.

CHARLES FLEMING is the coauthor of the *New York Times* bestseller *Three Weeks in October: The Manhunt for the Serial Sniper*. He is the author of the *Los Angeles Times* bestseller *High Concept: Don Simpson and the Hollywood Culture of Excess* and the novels *The Ivory Coast* and *After Havana*. He is a veteran entertainment reporter and columnist for such publications as *Newsweek*, *Variety*, and *Vanity Fair*, and an adjunct professor of journalism at the University of Southern California's Annenberg School for Communication. He lives with his wife and their two daughters in Los Angeles.